D0908606

Embers of Death

Also by Stella Shepherd

EMBERS OF DEATH
Stella Shepherd

St. Martin's Press ⚹ New York

EMBERS OF DEATH. Copyright © 1996 by Stella Shepherd.
All rights reserved. Printed in the United States of
America. No part of this book may be used or
reproduced in any manner whatsoever without written
permission except in the case of brief quotations
embodied in critical articles or reviews. For information,
address St. Martin's Press, 175 Fifth Avenue,
New York, N.Y. 10010.

Library of Congress Cataloging-in-Publication Data

Shepherd, Stella.
    Embers of death : an Inspector Montgomery
mystery / Stella Shepherd.
        p.   cm.
    ISBN 0-312-15097-0
    1. Montgomery, Richard (Fictitious character)—
Fiction.   I. Title.
PR6069.H454E45   1997
823'.914—dc20   96-44846
                                                      CIP

First published in Great Britain by
Constable & Company Ltd.

First U.S. Edition: January 1997

10 9 8 7 6 5 4 3 2 1

Embers of Death

1

'Young Radcliffe got a good send-off tonight,' commented Detective Inspector Richard Montgomery, guiding his Sierra along lamp-lit roads towards the area of Nottingham where his sergeant lived.

'Yes,' agreed William Bird, who was slumped in mellow contentment in the front passenger seat. 'He's a popular lad, and a hard worker. He'll do well in the new post.'

'Mm.' The spring night was mild, and Montgomery had opened his window two inches to enjoy the air; now his nostrils twitched slightly as a teasing smell of smoke entered the car.

'Thanks for driving,' went on Sergeant Bird. 'I enjoyed this evening.'

Montgomery smiled to himself. His friend's normally rosy complexion had been several shades richer when they had left DC Radcliffe's farewell party in the Red Lion. They had attended out of a sense of duty, but been pleasantly surprised to find few of the raucous excesses which had seemed inseparable from such parties in the past. Just one or two diehards like DS Jackson, and Rennie, his pal from the uniformed branch, still equated masculinity with volume of liquor consumed.

Montgomery himself, though not teetotal, found abstinence no great sacrifice. He welcomed society's strengthening cultural attitudes against drink-driving. If these had come five years earlier, perhaps William Bird would not now be a widower, victim of a stranger's selfishness, a man of forty-five going home to the company of his cat. Outwardly at least, he had accepted the blow with quiet courage; it was Montgomery, regarded as a cold fish by his juniors, who still experienced echoes of the white-hot flare of injustice he had felt at the time. If his own wife Carole had been killed in that way, he was sure that bitterness would have been his shadow for life . . .

They were now less than a mile from William Bird's roomy Edwardian terraced house, and the smell of smoke was becoming stronger. 'Perhaps someone's burning rubbish?' murmured the sergeant, levering his well-covered frame into a more erect position and peering through the windscreen. 'No . . . eleven o'clock's a bit late for that. Maybe a brazier's got out of control? There's a little park round here that's a favourite spot for some of our older ladies and gentlemen of the road.'

'There's another possibility.' Montgomery felt a feathery tingle in his scalp. 'It could be the work of – Look!' He glanced in the mirror, swung the wheel sharp left and accelerated up a side street bordering an open patch of land. Ahead, lurid flickerings gave staccato illumination to the ground floor of the end house in a run-down Victorian terrace. Parking the car abruptly, Montgomery was out and running before William Bird had begun to grapple with the seat belt.

A motley group of figures milled nearby. 'Has anyone rung for the fire brigade?' demanded Montgomery.

'Yes. They're on their way.'

'Any people inside?'

'No; these end two houses have been empty for a while.' The paunchy middle-aged man who was providing this information leapt back in alarm as the front window suddenly exploded with a fierce bang. The fire roared towards its new oxygen supply; flames licked out into the night, searing the brickwork above, probing with avid fingers at the thin glass of the bedroom window.

Montgomery, hand raised as a shield from the heat, became aware that Sergeant Bird had joined him. 'The house is unoccupied, apparently,' he began, then broke off as a thin keening sound reached his ears. 'What's that?' It came again. William Bird pointed upwards, where they saw with horror a strange ragged shape clawing at the first-floor window. Briefly the external flames illuminated a grimy face, the mouth straining wide as another cry struggled to prevail against the din of the inferno. Then the figure disappeared.

'It's an old woman,' gasped Montgomery. 'She must have gone to the back – or collapsed in the smoke.'

'The stairs open off the sitting-room,' supplied the local man. 'They'll be ablaze. She'll never get down that way.'

'Do you live near?'

'Four doors up.'

'You have a ladder?'

'No. My neighbour has, but he's away on holiday and he keeps it locked in his shed.'

Montgomery listened intently for the siren of the fire brigade; all he could hear was the spurting fury of the flames. 'We'll go round the back,' he said. 'Bring a torch, and some wet towels – as soon as you can. Oh, and a hammer or even a brick to smash the window.'

With Sergeant Bird at his heels, Montgomery hurried up the side passageway to the rear of the house. Here he was forced to move with more caution. Though the front of the terrace was a glaring mass of pyrotechnics, the back yard lay in deep shadow. Only the faintest reflections reached down into the black pit from the orange glow in the sky above. The two men picked their way towards the kitchen window, skirting a solid square structure which abutted the wall on the left. 'Coal bunker, I think,' said Montgomery, feeling the texture of concrete with his hand. 'This could be useful.' Through the smoke haze in the kitchen, a sinister flickering light was just visible around the door to the sitting-room; he prayed the door would hold firm a while longer.

The rear bedroom was in blackness. Montgomery scrambled on top of the coal bunker, shouting 'Hello!' at the blind window. There was no reply. He stretched towards the sill, but could barely brush it with his fingers. He could leap, and hang, but he was unlikely to gain entry that way. 'Something else to stand on!' he shouted at William Bird. 'Quick!'

'There's only the dustbin; it won't be very stable. Wait: our friend's coming.' A wavering torchlight bisected the yard; as Sergeant Bird explained their problem it swung promptly to a nearby pile of debris and they soon located a stout wooden crate.

'Here.' The man thrust the crate at Montgomery, who found he could now reach the window with its help. The window was locked. He beat a sharp tattoo on the pane, and continued to shout. Still there was no sign of life inside.

'I'm going in,' he told the shadowy figures below. 'Give me the towels.' He wiped his face, then slung them round his neck. 'Now the torch and whatever you've got for the glass.'

'Sir – if there's no one there . . .' Sergeant Bird was appalled. 'Let me go, sir. You've got Carole to think about, and the children.' He made as if to heave himself on to the coal bunker, but was firmly repulsed by Montgomery. 'Thanks, Will, but I stand a better chance.' It was undeniable. Montgomery was not only four years younger than his sergeant, but taller, slimmer and fitter. 'I've no intention of taking unnecessary risks,' he added.

'The fire brigade . . .'

' . . . aren't here.'

'I can hear something,' said their companion.

They listened. With the ear of faith, there was a faint wail of sirens, but it was far away across the city. 'They're probably dealing with another fire,' said Montgomery. 'Right. I'm off.' He shone the torch into the kitchen window, but the light was reflected back at him from the thick wall of smoke inside. He felt the pane; it was warm. Protecting his face with a towel, he weighed the hammer in his hand and prepared to swing it at the upper window.

'Sir!' William Bird's shout stopped him in mid-swing. 'Someone's coming to the window!'

Montgomery pulled the towel aside as a strange Medusa-

8

like apparition materialized from the swirling fumes and raised its arms as if in an incantation. Then came a click, and he realized that the old woman had managed to release the window lock. She sank to her knees, tugging feebly at the sash, but Montgomery was now able to strain it open from his side. He pulled himself over the sill and fell sprawling on to the floor beside her. His whooping breath was cut short by the sharp assault of acrid smoke. He spluttered and choked, and his eyes began to pour tears. Heat throbbed all around them. From behind the door to the landing came a low background roar punctuated by greedy crackles.

The air from the window seemed to have revived the old woman. As Montgomery rose to replenish his own supplies she was already there, leaning out eagerly. 'Where's the ladder?' she croaked.

'We don't have one. I'll help you over the sill, then you must jump. There are two men below who'll catch you.' He yelled instructions to Sergeant Bird and his companion. 'Now, is anyone else in this house?'

'No, sir. Just me.'

'Here we go, then.'

'No!' She dug desperate talons into his forearm. 'I can't do that! I can't!'

'If you stay here, you'll roast. We both shall.'

'Please . . . can't we wait for a ladder? I'm too old for jumping. You go. I'll wait here . . .' She doubled over in a hacking cough.

'There isn't *time!*' Montgomery's voice was rough. With a ladder he could have flung her over his shoulder in a fireman's lift, but as things were, the old woman's co-operation was vital.

'What's happening?' called William Bird from the yard below.

'She doesn't want to jump.' Montgomery felt stupefied by fumes and the knowledge that time was too short to embark on the path of reason he would normally have chosen.

'Lower her down,' instructed his sergeant calmly. 'If I stand

9

on the coal bunker I'll be able to catch her legs, and Reg here will stand at the bottom. Is that all right, Annie?'

The old woman, her entire face and body stiff with terror, suddenly cackled with glee. 'He knows my name!'

'Come on, Annie,' floated William Bird's voice from the beckoning night air. 'We won't let you be hurt.'

Miraculously, in less than a minute Montgomery was leaning out, bracing his back, gripping the thin bony wrists, passing the old lady like a roll of carpet to the willing helpers below. As he did so there was a reverberant crash behind him, and fire erupted into the room. It plucked at his clothing as he scrambled over the sill. For a few seconds he hung in cool darkness, then released his fingers and leapt to the terrace.

'It wasn't me,' gibbered Annie Bartholomew as she sat cocooned in a blanket, watching firemen competently direct high-pressure hoses into the near-gutted building. 'I had a candle, but it wasn't me. I was in that front bedroom, asleep. The door was ajar and I woke up coughing. There was fire on the ground floor – I couldn't go down the stairs. I went to the window ... all flames were coming up from the window below. I crouched at the back of the room, but then I knew I'd die if I stayed there. I crawled along the landing and into the back bedroom ... It wasn't me, honestly. I didn't start it. I've lost all my belongings in that house!'

'No one's accusing you, Annie,' soothed William Bird. His eyes met Montgomery's. 'Reckon it's another piece of work from our pyro, sir?'

Montgomery nodded. His ankle ached, but he was otherwise intact. If, like a cat, he had nine lives, then at least one had just been rendered forfeit. Belatedly, he scanned the thin crowd of onlookers who were watching the firemen from a safe distance. Was someone out there deriving more satisfaction from this drama than the rest? They were young men mostly, but there were also some middle-aged men and women, probably locals from the houses immediately adjacent. Someone should check out their identities before they all melted away . . .

By his side, Sergeant Bird was speaking once more to Annie Bartholomew. 'If the medics don't need to keep you overnight, we'll find you somewhere to stay,' he told her. 'I'm sure the Salvation Army hostel will manage something.'

Montgomery flicked his attention back to the pair and added his own reassurance. 'You'll be ready for a nice warm bath.'

'A *bath*?' she shrieked in outrage. 'Why should I want one of those?'

'All that smoke,' he said, indicating her dusky face.

Annie Bartholomew rose, drew her thin shoulders together, consulted the wing mirror of a nearby police patrol car and addressed him firmly. 'Sir,' she said, 'I'll have you know my face is *always* this colour!'

'Friday's fire in Bishop Street was the seventh in our series of unexplained conflagrations,' Montgomery told his squad of detectives on the Monday. 'As you know, the first was January fifteenth in Mapperley, and every subsequent fire has occurred to the east of Nottingham, in the city or suburbs, with one exception.'

'The haystack,' put in DS Jackson.

'That's right. I think we need to treat that one warily, as a possible case of spontaneous combustion. There's evidence that the fire started in the *centre* of the stack. Leaving out the solitary rural case, then, we have had six to analyse – and a pattern *has* emerged.' He moved to the wall, where William Bird had drawn up a chronological chart of events. 'First, the sites chosen for the fires: always empty properties. In four cases these were unoccupied houses, in one case a derelict shed, and in another the office building of an abandoned factory was partially destroyed. In all six cases the agent used was thought by fire investigators to be paraffin. Combustible materials were deliberately stacked in one area, a corner of the ground floor, and ignited.

'The fires were all started mid-to-late evening, but there is no consistency in terms of days of the week. We have a Tuesday, two Thursdays, two Fridays and a Saturday. The most notable finding is the frequency pattern. Five weeks between the first and second fires, four and a half weeks between the second and third – then a significant acceleration leading to the latest gap of only ten days. You'll appreciate the relationship isn't linear . . . it's virtually exponential!'

As they murmured, he went on, 'That, for me, is the most worrying feature. So what can we infer from the information we've got so far?'

'The motive doesn't appear to be either personal grudge or connected with insurance claims,' said Graham Smythe, a doe-eyed DC who found the psychology of human relationships fascinating, despite his own sparse experience in this field.

'I don't think motive is much of a problem,' scoffed Jackson. 'It's kids – vandals, doing it for a bit of excitement.'

'Why do you say that, Brian?' asked Montgomery.

'Well, in the case of that shed, wasn't some glue-sniffing paraphernalia found? And hadn't a gang of boys been seen there on and off during the weeks before the fire?'

'Would you burn down your own den?' mused Sergeant Bird.

'You might if you'd found a better one.' Jackson was defiant.

'Could that particular fire have been an accident?' asked Smythe. 'You know, cigarettes?'

'No,' said Montgomery. 'The forensic evidence clearly pointed to arson. But Brian *could* be on the right track. William and I had some passing involvement in the aftermath of Friday's fire . . .' He sent a sharp warning glance towards Sergeant Bird, who had been threatened with tortures too grotesque to name if he dared to divulge the full story.' . . . and there were certainly some young lads among the spectators. Old Annie, the vagrant who almost perished, told us some interesting things. She likes to "move house", as she

12

calls it, every few months, and she had taken up residence in Bishop Street in March. At first she slept downstairs, but when "some boys" started playing around in the other empty house next door she decided to transfer her few belongings up to the front bedroom to reduce the chance of being robbed. She says that one evening last week she heard noises directly below her, and wondered if these same boys were responsible. She was seriously considering moving out when the arsonist intervened.'

'What happened exactly?' asked Jackson.

'She went to sleep early in the front bedroom – about eight o'clock, she reckons. She had obtained a bottle of brandy that day, and had been sampling it since late afternoon. Luckily, she awoke coughing with smoke and when she found that the ground floor was ablaze she was able to escape with some assistance through the back bedroom window.'

'There's no chance she started the fire herself?'

'None at all.'

When lines of enquiry had been discussed and tasks allocated, Graham Smythe took down a volume from the shelf near his desk and began to leaf through the index. From his own desk nearby Jackson heard a series of huffs of annoyance.

'What's wrong?' he asked at last.

'This is supposed to cover every aspect of forensic psychiatry. I've looked up "pyromania" – nothing. I tried "fire" – again, nothing.'

'How about "arson"? Or would that be too esoteric?'

Smythe's thin poetic cheeks briefly flared with pink as he scrabbled again among the leaves.

'Big word for you, Brian,' commented William Bird cheerfully, drawing up his chair.

'He picks them up from you,' muttered Smythe, still avoiding their eyes.

Sergeant Bird gave a genial smile. 'Read out what you find, Graham. It might help us get a handle on a suspect.'

'Er, yes . . . okay. Let's see . . . Arson. Property offence, destructive . . . Er, there are two broad subgroups: fire as a means to an end, or cases where the fire itself is the focus of interest. In the first group you've got situations like insurance fraud, or part-time firemen creating work for themselves – yes, honestly! – or people covering up the evidence of a crime. Then there are politically motivated fires, and gang activities . . .'

'Kids showing off to each other,' stated Jackson. 'Kudos within the gang. Mark my words, that'll be the reason.'

'Any more, Graham?' asked Sergeant Bird.

'Yes. Hang on . . . er, personal revenge, "cry for help", and finally inadequates who relish all the commotion they cause, or want an opportunity to play the hero.'

'What about the group where the end point is the fire itself?'

'Well, some are individuals responding to an irresistible impulse, a small number have an actual fire fetish . . .' At his side, Jackson snorted. '. . . and the rest are firesetting to relieve feelings of tension or depression.' Smythe closed the book and raised his gaze to Sergeant Bird. 'Some of those subgroups overlap, and some reflect underlying states, like schizophrenia, but in many of the categories the perpetrator can be perfectly sane.'

'Sane or not,' said William Bird, 'whoever is responsible must be caught soon. There was almost a tragedy on Friday night. Next time, someone could be killed.'

2

There was definitely something furtive about the boy in the shop. Margaret Kendall could see him in the security mirror, glancing to right and left, now up the short aisle towards the dispensing area, now down to the window behind which his friends were milling in feigned nonchalance. Across the

14

counter Mrs Goldsmith, a longstanding customer, was divulging a detailed confessional about skin eruptions on her hands and other complaints in less mentionable places.

Margaret herself was only an assistant at Furlong End Pharmacy, but many of their patrons, women especially, liked to discuss their medical problems with her in preference to Robert or Judy. Robert, the proprietor and qualified pharmacist, was too dry and precise for many people's taste, while Judy, like her recent predecessor, carried the stigma of youth. Forty-three-year-old Margaret, known in the district to have nursed her sick father for years, was a natural choice for older customers seeking advice.

'This moisturising cream should help the general dryness,' she told Mrs Goldsmith. 'It's hypoallergenic, no perfume or known irritants . . . You might like to try a mild hydrocortisone cream for the more specific patches of dermatitis. Just a thin smear, twice a day. Don't use it for longer than a fortnight, and never use it on your face . . .' She gave further instructions, her eyes flicking periodically to the mirror. Robert and Judy were filling prescriptions in the small dispensary, as the boy was well aware. Now he was picking up a bottle of aftershave and peering around again.

'Thank you,' Mrs Goldsmith was enthusing. 'You might be right about the rubber gloves. Now I come to think of it, I'm sure my hands are worse when I've had a good cleaning session. I'll try cotton inners, like you suggest . . .' Margaret nodded, briskly completed the transaction and checked the mirror one more time. Now she recognized the boy as Glenn, the son of one of her neighbours and normally a pleasant, studious boy. As she watched, he appeared to thrust the bottle into his trouser pocket.

Margaret stepped out from behind the counter, then hesitated. She wasn't entirely sure of what she had seen, and more unpleasantness was the last thing Robert needed just now. It was only six weeks since he had been forced to sack his previous pharmacy assistant for robbing the till. That had been traumatic for everyone. As for Glenn, if this was an isolated lapse, perhaps the shock of near-detection would prove a future deterrent.

She coughed, slowly skirted a cosmetics display and smiled enquiringly down the aisle at the boy. 'Can I help you with something, Glenn, or are you just browsing?'

'Er . . .' The bottle was back in his hands now, and his neck was mottled. 'Just having a look, Miss Kendall. Er, deciding.'

'The aftershave?'

'Er, I don't think, er . . .' He replaced it on the shelf. 'Thank you.' He turned and shambled outside, where his friends were waiting. A tall boy with a scarlet necktie asked a question. Glenn shook his head. The boy sneered.

There was no time to brood, as she heard a little laugh from the dispensary, and Judy's clear young voice making a jocular comment. The sound carried across the now empty shop, and Margaret felt herself stiffen. Robert and Judy got on well together. She should be glad, but . . .

'We've done Mr Sely's prescription, all seven items.' Judy, an attractive girl of nineteen, stepped out into the shop, her blonde pony-tail swinging. 'Is he coming back today?'

'Yes. He's just gone to the fruit shop.'

'Right-ho. Quiet, isn't it? Would you like a cup of tea?'

'*I'll* make it.' Margaret walked determinedly to the discreet staircase leading to their rest room on the first floor. *She* knew best how Robert preferred his tea . . . 'You don't want to be cooped up in the back all day, Judy. Why not mind the shop for a bit when I come down?'

'Fair enough.' Judy was always equable, co-operative. One couldn't dislike her, but Margaret begrudged the time she was spending in cosy sessions with Robert, learning about the properties of medicines and the techniques of dispensing, in a way she had never begrudged the previous assistant, Andrew. It had been nice to work with two men. She had felt special then.

Business was sluggish throughout the afternoon. In the cramped dispensary Robert leafed through a set of accounts, the long brow beneath his thinning hair furrowed in concen-

16

tration, short-sighted eyes peering through steel-rimmed spectacles. He was five years younger than Margaret, but a build-up of recent anxieties had made him look fifty. She longed to touch his shoulder, but refrained; he didn't like physical contact.

It was a relief when Dr Huxtable strode through the door at four o'clock. Florid and ebullient, he worked both at the District Hospital and at the nearby private Grange Hospital; every now and then he came to Furlong End for personal patent medicines.

'Hello there, Robert,' he boomed as the pharmacist emerged. 'I want something for my wife's cough: something with an expectorant.' As Robert turned to the shelf, he went on, 'I see you've succumbed.'

'I beg your pardon?'

'Those herbal remedies you weren't going to stock at any price . . . I must say that's a striking display in your window.'

'I didn't have much choice.' Robert's voice was bleak. 'They're advertised in all the ladies' magazines.'

'Got to earn a living, I suppose,' nodded Huxtable. 'Still, the manufacturers of Calm Night and Serenity are lucky to have such ready outlets. If they had to undergo the same rigorous tests as prescription-only medicines – the clinical trials, the statistical analyses – they wouldn't survive to be sold anywhere. But by classifying themselves as food supplements they avoid the regulations.'

'Without retail pharmacies, they'd merely sell by mail order.' Margaret tried to keep the defensive anger out of her voice. She knew what it had cost Robert to oppose his own instincts on this particular issue; she hated to see him scratching around for new areas of trade, however peripheral. Wasn't Dr Huxtable aware that after years of buying theatre supplies from Furlong End, his precious Grange Hospital had just awarded its new contract elsewhere? Behind her in the stock room were six useless boxes of anaesthetic drugs, a complete white elephant for a community pharmacy. No, she thought with a sigh, he wouldn't know. He was a surgeon,

17

this was a pharmaceutical matter. 'We feel that if the patients believe in them, they're doing some good.'

'Patients believe, all right,' conceded Huxtable. 'Anything with "natural" or "herbal" in the title. There's a case in point, a lady we've been seeing in the Joint Oncology Clinic. She's got recurrent breast cancer, oestrogen receptor positive. We put her on Tamoxifen two months ago, a specific treatment, and by chance she started the Bath and Wells raw vegetable diet at exactly the same time. I saw her again yesterday. Tremendous improvement. The chest wall lesions were half the size, and she felt really well in herself . . . I leave you to guess where she imagines the credit lies. The danger is, she was all for throwing away the Tamoxifen!'

He dug in his pocket for coins, and paid for the linctus. 'How is Theresa?' he asked.

Margaret's interest in the conversation evaporated. She didn't want to hear the ridiculous warmth that always came into Robert's voice whenever he discussed his insipid little wife. She turned her attention to the thin, unhealthy-looking young man just coming in at the door; Judy had disappeared to the bathroom.

'This, please,' he mumbled, placing a tube of toothpaste on the counter. 'Oh – and this.' The apparent afterthought was a prescription for Diconal, an opioid analgesic; as a Controlled Drug, it was subject to stringent prescription requirements.

She took the paper with a half-smile and indicated the row of seats where he could wait. 'It'll be a few minutes,' she said. Dr Huxtable was just leaving. 'Prescription for you, Mr McPherson,' she said brightly to Robert.

As soon as they were together in the dispensary she put a finger to her lips, then pulled a face. He studied the script and nodded. Only days before, they had received warning that a batch of FP10 forms had been stolen from a GP surgery in central Nottingham. Although this form had been completed in accordance with the necessary criteria – quantities written in words and figures, plus the other safeguards – both felt

18

instinctively that it was suspect. 'I'll ring the surgery from upstairs,' whispered Robert, 'then the police if it's not above board. Try to keep him here.' He glided out to the shop, Margaret at his shoulder. 'I haven't got quite enough of these,' he told the youth, 'but I believe some more came with the new stock. I'll just go and check.'

The young man subsided, looking uneasy, and Margaret proceeded to serve two teenage girls who were choosing mascara. She chatted with them amiably; the more relaxed the prevailing atmosphere, the less likely the boy was to bolt. When Judy returned from the small lavatory next to the ground-floor stock room, there was no opportunity to explain the situation, but Margaret considered that no bad thing: Judy might lack the necessary acting prowess.

After fifteen minutes, the youth appeared at the counter. 'What's going on?' he asked truculently. 'Why is it taking so long?'

'I'm sorry. I'm sure Mr McPherson is doing his best. The boxes were in a bit of a jumble when they were delivered. He has to check things like batch numbers and expiry dates . . .' She turned to Judy. 'What were you laughing about before? Was it that script where Dr Brown wrote "Trampoline" instead of "Tranxene"?'

'Yes: we reckoned the patient would be bouncing with health.'

'I think I'll go and buy a paper,' muttered the boy. 'I'll come back later for the medicines.'

'Let me just show you – Oh! Here's Mr McPherson now.'

'Everything is sorted out,' said Robert. He attempted a smile, but to Margaret it looked more like a nervous tic. 'We have the requisite quantity. I shall dispense them now.'

More delay followed. Margaret felt her stomach tighten. The shop was empty, and the boy was glaring suspiciously towards the dispensary. She could hear the swish of cars on the road outside. Where *were* the police? Why didn't they hurry?

'Have you a minute, Margaret?' called Robert from behind her. 'The labelling computer seems to be playing up . . .'

The boy's lips tightened, and he turned on his heel. Head down, he ran towards the door. At the last moment a solid navy blue figure loomed on the other side and there was nowhere to go.

'Where were you off to in such a hurry?' asked the constable as the youth cowered against a shelf. 'I'm afraid we need a few minutes of your time. What's your name?'

A mumble.

'What's that again?'

'I said, Sean Turner.'

'Well now, Mr Turner, let's find out what you've been up to.'

It didn't take long. Another officer arrived, and soon Sean Turner was dragging reluctant feet towards the doorway, a thin slice of turkey in a hearty blue sandwich. To the pharmacy staff, watching with a flutter of excited fear from the back of the shop, there was sullen defeat in his every movement. But suddenly they had a shock. At the last moment he tore one arm from the grasp of his captors and whirled round.

He stared straight at Robert, chill malevolence in his deep-set eyes. 'You little weasel,' he hissed, 'you think you're so clever. Don't think I don't know. But I'll get you. Just you wait. I'll do it. I'll get you . . .'

Geoff Crabbe swaggered towards The Flower Bower and peered inside past the window display. So the old dragon was in occupation – no problem! He'd go round the back and take a shufti.

In the yard at the rear of the shop, he dropped his smouldering cigarette and ground it beneath his shoe. Passing a stack of boxes, he slid through the open back door into a large, cool room full of woody and floral scents. The air was moist and the light seemed dim after the power of the sun outside – but not too dim to make out the neat shape of the woman across the room.

She was completely unaware of his presence. She stood at a bench, deftly clipping carnation stalks, arranging the blooms in bunches and wrapping them in transparent paper. For half a minute, he simply watched. Then he padded forward and placed both hands on her shoulders. "Ello, darlin'," he whispered.

She jumped and gasped. 'Geoff!'

'Shh. You don't want Hecate out there to hear.'

'What can I do for you?'

He avoided making the suggestive answer he would have given Shona; these were early days. 'I just came to check that tomorrow is still on.'

She studied him gravely, head slightly to one side. She had pale blue eyes and short, wavy black hair, a combination which interested and attracted him. 'I did say yes.'

'True enough. Well . . . let's say I just wanted to see you again. It's no good me bringin' flowers here – coals to Newcastle, an' all that – so I brought you something else.'

'Oh – you shouldn't have.'

'But I did.' He took a brown paper bag from his pocket and offered it to her with a flourish. 'Here – with my undying esteem.'

'Grapes! Thank you!' She giggled, then bit her lip, glancing towards the entry to the shop where her employer was engaged with a customer.

'We can get on to the hardware later.'

'You are silly – but thanks again.'

'Until tomorrow, then.' He bowed and sauntered off, pausing in the yard to light another cigarette. The sharp snip of secateurs followed him out into the sunshine . . . then he heard her low, melodic humming.

3

The car-park at Newstead Abbey was a gentle grassy slope overlooking the eastern end of a large, sparkling lake.

'I'm glad we could drag you out,' said Carole Montgomery to William Bird as they strolled down the incline towards the ruins of the poet Byron's old home. 'The air's so lovely. It's a crime to sit at home on a bright Sunday reading books.'

'I agree,' said her husband fervently, and they laughed. It was a longstanding joke between them that Montgomery read few books, and never classics, while his sergeant did little else. 'Literary references don't catch criminals,' Montgomery was wont to claim, while Carole, with the substantial advantage of being a former English teacher, would counter that work wasn't everything and a knowledge of one's literary heritage made one a more complete person. Today, with their teenaged children out riding with friends, they had an opportunity to blend heritage with exercise.

As the mellow stonework of the Abbey's west front came into view, Carole paused to marvel. 'I always found this architecture curious when I was a girl,' she said. 'On the left a great empty window, clearly a religious artefact from medieval times, on the right a sort of Norman tower with battlements, and linking them a building which looks distinctly Tudor, also with mock battlements! But the guidebook explains it all. There was a priory here first, which was dissolved at the Reformation. The estate was granted to Sir John Byron of Colwick, who used the priory buildings to form the basis of his family mansion: the whole lot became known as Newstead Abbey.'

'His descendants ran into debt, though,' said Sergeant Bird. 'They couldn't maintain it.'

'That's right. The Abbey was so neglected that large chunks were uninhabitable by the time the famous Byron, the sixth baron, gained his inheritance. Even the good bits were gloomy and gothic. Eventually he was forced to sell.'

' "Huge halls, long galleries, spacious chambers, joined by no quite lawful marriage of the arts . . ." ' quoted William Bird. 'He wrote that in *Don Juan*.'

Montgomery strode ahead in case his sergeant felt the urge to quote any more. Though it was only mid-morning, Newstead was filling up with people eager to enjoy its broad grounds . . . Suddenly he heard a sinister rustling sound directly above. Startled, he ducked down as a huge dark creature like an albatross flapped clumsily over his head.

'Cor, 'strewth,' came a voice from nearby. Montgomery continued to watch the big bird, a peacock, as it appeared to be heading for an undignified crash-landing against the wall of the building just below the mock battlements; at the last minute it soared upwards to alight safely on a stone ledge, delighting the crowd.

Montgomery turned to the person who had spoken, a brown-haired man of forty dressed in flashy casuals. 'Geoff,' he said. 'Long time no see. How are you?'

'Not so bad, Mr Montgomery,' he leered. 'And yourself?'

'Ticking over, thank you. How's business?'

The leer became broader. 'Booming.'

'What are you into these days?'

Crabbe watched another peacock desperately flapping to gain some altitude. 'I didn't know those buggers could fly,' he muttered. 'What am I into? A bit o' this, a bit o' that. You know me. Buying and selling. Imports, distribution . . . Earning an honest crust.'

Montgomery raised an ironic eyebrow. 'That's good news. And how's your wife?'

'Monica is fine, thank you.'

'Is she here with you?'

'Not today.'

Montgomery nodded and bade him a cordial farewell, inwardly amused. Geoff Crabbe could be considered a man of some substance these days, with multiple small business interests. He was also a fence and a womanizer – a hopeless recidivist on both counts. Perhaps his presence here at Newstead signalled an assignation? One thing Montgomery knew . . . Crabbe hadn't come here to bone up on Byron.

Robert and Theresa McPherson left the vivid reds and yellows of the Spanish Garden and meandered to the Eagle Pond, a large rectangular pool lush with plant fronds and mysterious grey fish.

'I think it's touching that Byron cared so much for his dog,' ventured Theresa, referring to a monument they had just passed. 'I read once that he would have been buried here with Boatswain himself if he hadn't been forced to sell the property.'

'Mm.' Robert was not interested in dogs, cats or any other animals. Smelly, unhygienic creatures . . . he couldn't understand a man becoming so besotted with his pet that he would arrange for such an elaborate memorial. It seemed unhealthy to him.

'There has probably been a pond at this site from the time of the original priory,' he said, primly changing the subject. 'At the Dissolution, a brass eagle lectern was thrown into the water, then recovered two centuries later. Hence the name, Eagle Pond. That's the lectern we've seen in Southwell Minster . . .' He frowned, suddenly reminded of his mother by mention of Southwell. She lived in a village close to the attractive Nottinghamshire town, and he knew it was his duty to visit her again in the near future. He consulted his watch. 'Perhaps I should make time to see Mother this afternoon.'

'Oh, please don't. Not today.' Theresa reached for his arm, but he shrugged her off, as he always did.

'It's been ten days. And since Father died . . .'

'I know. But it's so lovely here, it would be a shame to hurry back. We've been looking forward to this outing all week . . . You could see her one evening – or what about next Saturday?'

He considered. Theresa would be working in The Flower Bower all day, but the pharmacy would close at lunch time. Saturday would give him an opportunity to sort through some more of his father's belongings in the bedroom and attic. 'Perhaps,' he said.

Slowly they walked along the edge of the tranquil pool. Over by the exit to the Tropical Gardens, a man appeared to be staring at them. 'Is that someone you know?' hissed Robert to his wife.

24

'Who? Oh – him. No, I don't think so. Why?'

'He's been watching us. It's really most insolent. Wait – he's coming over.'

'Mr McPherson?'

'Yes?'

'I'm Geoff Crabbe. We've spoken on the telephone.'

Robert stiffened. Before, there had just been a voice. An unctuous voice he had mistrusted. Now he was being subjected to the voice's flesh and blood owner. He saw a slim man with a swagger, his own age or a little older, with an incipient paunch masked by a ludicrous snakeskin belt. The chunky gold signet ring on the little finger of his right hand winked a brash message; behind the easy grin his teeth looked pointed, slightly cruel. 'How did you know my identity?' he asked.

Crabbe made an expansive gesture. 'You're in retail, on public display . . .'

'. . . During business hours,' finished Robert icily. 'I don't conduct business during a Sunday stroll with my wife.'

'Ah – this must be the lovely Theresa. Good morning!'

There was alarm in her eyes as she stammered a reply. Robert gratefully clutched at the protective anger this triggered: it helped to combat the flickers of fear. 'Stay here, Theresa,' he instructed. 'Mr Crabbe and I will just be a few minutes.' He led the way to the other side of the pond, then turned on the interloper. 'I told you last week I want nothing to do with your proposals.'

'You didn't let me explain them fully, but you should. Andrew is sure we can make a deal of mutual benefit.'

'Andrew!' Robert almost spat in his contempt. 'I wouldn't be a party to anything that worthless little thief presumes to mediate if it paid me.'

'That's just the point – it *will* pay you. Handsomely.'

'Unlicensed drugs from dubious foreign factories? No, thank you.'

'*Cheap* drugs. Your patients won't know the difference. They still get the medicine they need . . . everyone's happy.'

25

'I said no. I can't make it any plainer than that.'

Disconcertingly, Geoff Crabbe merely grinned again. He produced a gold-plated lighter, lit a cigarette, and stood in an atti- tude of contemplative relaxation while Robert's solar plexus twanged with unease. For almost a minute, no words were exchanged. He was aware of Theresa watching them anxiously from across the water.

The silence became too much. 'I'll repeat my answer,' Robert said, his voice a few tones higher. 'I'm not interested. That is my final word on the matter.'

He turned as if to sever the conversation, but Crabbe fell into step beside him. 'You're assuming', he said smoothly, 'that you have a choice.'

Robert stopped. 'What do you mean?'

Crabbe was in no hurry to reply. He inhaled the acrid smoke twice, slowly, before making another of his affable gestures. 'Andrew told me some fascinating things about the goings-on in your pharmacy.'

'Goings-on?'

'That's right. Try this for size: patient comes in and pays one or more prescription fees for the items you dispense – lot of dosh, that, these days. Then you scribble on the back of the form and pretend they were exempt from charge . . . you with me? And you claim for the money you apparently didn't receive.'

'What you're describing is fraud. And that has no relevance to Furlong End Pharmacy.'

'Maybe not now. But it did have, didn't it? That's one of the reasons you sacked Andrew. But you didn't take the matter any further because you knew it would be difficult to prove that *he* was the miscreant. Especially considering it had been going on for four years. And mud sticks, doesn't it? People would start to have their doubts about Furlong End –'

'I don't wish to discuss this with you. My relationship with a former employee is no concern of yours.'

'Oh, but it is. Andrew works for me now, and we have valid ideas for mutual benefit. Furlong End can only gain.'

'I'm not interested.'

Crabbe smiled again, feigning weary exasperation, but his eyes looked narrow, ratty. The pupils seemed very small in the glare of the sun. 'Your wife,' he said. 'Pretty woman, isn't she? Like those flowers she arranges. I wouldn't want her to be . . . *bothered* . . . with any of this . . .'

Robert gasped. For a moment he wanted to hit out at his sneering tormentor. They were of similar height and build: one push and the man could be thrashing in the Eagle Pond . . . but caution prevailed. There was something sinister about Crabbe. He would not give up easily. He had at least one undesirable henchman. He had gone to some trouble to ensure that this meeting took place . . .

With a rush of increased horror Robert realized that he and Theresa must have been followed to Newstead that morning. It was outrageous. And Crabbe knew where Theresa worked. Alone, she was vulnerable to heaven knew what. 'Leave my wife out of this,' he stammered.

'I'd prefer to. What do you propose?'

'Ring me again at the shop during the week. I'll let you know then.'

'Very good.' Gold flashed again as Crabbe raised his hand to acknowledge Theresa on the distant bank. Then, with a nod at Robert, he was gone.

'You're *reading*!' accused Carole the following Saturday afternoon.

'That's right,' said Montgomery calmly.

'What's brought this on? Sunstroke?'

He adjusted his position in the garden chair beneath the willow tree. 'I'm always prepared to listen to my betters. You and Will have been banging on for long enough, saying what a philistine I am . . . I thought a bit of self-education was called for.'

She leaned into the shade to peer at the title. '*Lord of the Flies*. Ah, you got that from my shelf. Why that one?'

27

'Well, I didn't fancy anything depressing, so that excluded Thomas Hardy, I didn't want tales of poverty in Victorian London, so that let Dickens out, or irony in Regency drawing-rooms, so no Jane Austen, or gothic melodramas, so no Brontë books . . . it was quite easy, really. I eventually narrowed the choice down to three: *Moby Dick*, *Three Men in a Boat*, and *Lord of the Flies*. The first looked heavy going, the second I'd already read – so here we are with William Golding. Reading about schoolboys stranded on a desert island is just right for hot weather. I can struggle and burn with them . . . then go and have a nice cold tomato juice.'

'It's allegorical,' she warned.

'Allegorical?'

'Well – it's not just an adventure story. It's a kind of metaphor. Golding was looking at wider moral and philosophical issues than just a tale of two parties of boys on an island.'

'Are you sure?' Montgomery looked doubtfully at the paperback. Perhaps he had made the wrong choice after all.

'Definitely. It was written in the early fifties, in the aftermath of World War II, when both political extremism and existentialist thought still prevailed – that is, anti-Christian nihilism.'

'Stop. I'm regretting my actions. Where's the lawn mower? I'll do the front lawn right now.'

She restrained him. 'Sorry. It's the teacher in me, bursting for an outlet. You read and interpret it in your own way – just tell me afterwards what you think.'

He sighed and subsided; she padded across the grass. 'Carole?'

'Yes?'

'Any chance of a tomato juice?'

'With ice and Worcestershire sauce?'

'Yes, please.'

'I dare say there might be – if that front lawn will be cut by tonight.'

Drat! 'It's a deal.'

It was only nine fifteen when Judy headed back home from her evening out. Phil, her boyfriend, was coming down with a cold, and had been poor company during their Cantonese meal. At least she had the independence of her own little Fiat: she had deposited Phil in his flat with all appropriate creature comforts, and was now cruising through Nottingham's outer suburbs on her way to the home ohe shared with her parents.

The most direct route took her past the pharmacy. Furlong End was walking distance from home both for Judy herself and for Margaret, which saved parking problems. The shop was situated at the end of a modern terrace, a small parade of similar retail premises, with only limited parking space for staff behind. The car-park used by customers, a 'Max Headroom' fifty yards or so up the road, seemed to attract various aimless youths, in pairs or groups; Judy never left her precious Fiat there.

As she drew near to the pharmacy, she could see that one such gang had congregated nearby, just outside the newsagent's. Instinctively she slowed the car. Furlong End would be fully secured, of course, with its special combination locks and the metal grille over the front door and windows, but the attention of the boys seemed to be directed towards the pharmacy – indeed, one of them was now pointing his finger.

She edged past as slowly as she dared and glanced across at her place of work. It was dusk, streetlamps were lit – and a light was glowing in the dispensary at the back of the shop. Had one of their confederates broken in?

As two of the boys peered in through the window, another member of the gang turned to look at her. Smartly she pressed her foot down and accelerated up the road, but minutes later she was creeping back down the other side. Now the group was loitering half-way down the precinct. Should she ring . . . no, wait. Suddenly a woman Judy recognized had emerged from the gloom. She walked purposefully up the side of the shop to the small concrete courtyard at the rear, then vanished. Judy gripped the wheel uncertainly. The light must mean that Robert was in there – all well and good. But did he know about the boys? They hadn't gone very far away, and she still felt apprehensive.

She sat in the Fiat, deciding what to do next.

The telephone bell jangled insistently; Montgomery sat up in the bed, rubbing his eyes, and flicked on his bedside lamp. 3 a.m! No wonder he felt like a husk. He reached out for the receiver. 'Hello, Montgomery.'

'Sir . . . It's Smythe, sir. I'm sorry to disturb you.'

'Go ahead, Graham.'

'I didn't know whether to ring you now, or leave it till tomorrow, but . . . there's been another suspicious fire.'

'You're sure?'

'Yes, sir. This one was in Furlong End – a retail pharmacy at the end of a row of shops. The blaze was very fierce; the building was virtually gutted. But that's not all . . . the proprietor is missing, sir. His wife says he never came home last night.'

4

'Bad news, isn't it, sir?'

Smythe quietly joined Montgomery as he surveyed the desolate, still-smoking ruin that had been Furlong End Pharmacy. The morning was cool and grey, and somewhere towards the city a church bell was tolling; it seemed a fitting appurtenance to the grim discovery of a blackened body in the charred wreckage minutes earlier.

'The worst.' It was a find everyone had dreaded. Whether or not the savagely burnt corpse proved to be that of the missing pharmacist – and identification would take serious effort –

someone had died here in the flames, and Montgomery felt a sick sense of responsibility.

'Perhaps this fire wasn't our arsonist at all,' said Smythe. 'Maybe it was an accident, or an attempt at insurance fraud.'

'It's possible . . .' Montgomery focused his mind with an effort. 'Tell me about Mrs McPherson – what was the story with her?'

'She was at home when HQ telephoned in the small hours to inform her husband that his shop was on fire. She'd waited up for him till eleven, then fallen asleep over her book in bed. It was a shock for her to find he still wasn't home. It seems he had gone to spend the afternoon with his widowed mother and had said he might stay on for dinner, but he was never in the habit of staying away all night.'

'I see. Well – she'll have to be told of this discovery.'

'Ros Winger is on duty at the station, sir.'

'Good.'

An hour later Ian May, the youthful local GP who doubled as police surgeon, was completing his preliminary examination at the site. He made a few brief notes on his dictaphone, then packed it away and turned to Montgomery with a sad shrug. 'I can't tell you much at this stage,' he said. 'Only the full PM will confirm whether the fire itself was the actual cause of death.'

Smythe, who had retreated to the edge of the debris on first sight of the human remains, now picked his way cautiously towards them. 'It's definitely a man?' he asked.

'Yes.'

'He looks as if he's been slugged over the head.'

There was an ugly ten-centimetre crack over the left side of the brittle scalp; through the gaping defect they could see damage to the skull beneath. 'Not necessarily,' said Ian May. 'You can get the scalp splitting because of heat contracture, and likewise skull fractures may result purely from the fire. I'm sure Prof Frobisher will do his best to distinguish fire damage from ante-mortem violence. As for this poor chap's identity . . . I expect they'll need dental records for confirmation. There are very few external clues.'

31

'Just a mutilated watch,' agreed Montgomery, 'and what's left of his glasses.'

Smythe pointed to a smoke-blackened receptacle near the corpse's right hand. 'That's a sort of cup. Bit small, though. Perhaps he'd been drinking Turkish coffee . . .'

'May I remove the watch?' Montgomery asked Ian May. 'Mrs McPherson might be able to recognize some part of it.'

'Go ahead. Use this pair of gloves.'

The watch seemed to cling to the friable skin at the wrist. Only with some difficulty was Montgomery able to perform his revolting task, and he was thankful when at last he could slide the ruined timepiece into a bag. Its face was unreadable, a melted distortion of metal and glass. But the back . . . suddenly Montgomery realized that the watch was inscribed. With mounting anticipation he rubbed at it with his handkerchief; the tiny symbols became clearer.

There was a date some seventeen years previously, then a few words in a flowing italic script. ' "*Robert*",' he read. ' "*21st birthday wishes from Mother and Father.*" '

It was some hours before Montgomery, now joined by Sergeant Bird, saw Theresa McPherson himself. Her small, modern house was almost obsessionally neat, its wooden surfaces highly polished, the furniture symmetrical, no stray papers marring the perfection. Only the ubiquitous floral arrangements in pristine cut-glass vases struggled for free expression: behind conventional clusters of roses and freesias, laurel twigs stretched like slender arms towards the light.

Theresa sat hunched on the sofa, her face white and tear-stained.

'She's very shocked,' murmured WPC Winger. 'Go easy on her, sir.' She effected the introductions, then returned to her seat next to the stricken woman.

'I'm sorry we have to disturb you at this time, Mrs McPherson,' said Montgomery. 'Please accept our sincere condolences for the loss of your husband. What we'd like to do is to make some sense out of what has happened. Do you think you could manage to answer just a few questions?'

She nodded. 'I'll try.'

'Thank you. Our initial investigations seem to indicate that the fire started some time between eleven and twelve o'clock. Have you any idea at all why Robert would be in the pharmacy so late on a Saturday night?'

'No.'

'Was he in the habit of working out of hours? Checking stock, perhaps, or going through accounts?'

'Not really. He was very methodical. He liked to keep things under control, keep regular hours. Sometimes he would choose to spend Saturday afternoons at the computer here in his study.'

'Is that linked to the one in the shop?'

'Yes.'

'Do you know if the business was doing well?'

'I – er, he didn't discuss the details with me. He didn't say it wasn't. We've always seemed to get by . . .' She lifted her head and stared round the room, as if seeing it with new eyes. 'Robert handled most of our bills.'

'Do you have a joint bank account?'

'Yes, but . . . I hardly ever look at the statements.'

'Presumably the shop was mortgaged?'

'Yes. Er, Lloyds Bank.'

'Thank you. How long has he owned the business?'

'Nine years. Before that he worked as a manager in someone else's pharmacy.'

'And how long have you been married, Mrs McPherson?'

Theresa's lip trembled; Ros Winger sent Montgomery a warning look.

'Seven years,' she answered thickly.

'Do you have children?'

'No.'

'Who else worked with your husband? Could you give me their names?'

'There's Margaret, Margaret Kendall. She's been with Robert since the beginning. And Judy, a young girl. Er, Judy

Pearce. She's quite new; she was taken on when the previous assistant, Andrew, had to leave about two months ago.'

'Was there friction between any of the current staff?'

'Not that Robert ever told me.'

'Fair enough. Just one more thing, if you don't mind . . . When Robert didn't come home last night, where did you believe he was?' Montgomery already knew the answer to this, but he wanted to hear her own words.

Her pale eyes seemed to darken. 'I thought he was with Honour.'

'Honour?'

'His mother. She lives in the village of Bramton, near Southwell. He visits her regularly now she's a widow.' Unconsciously she was using the present tense.

'Did you try to telephone when it was getting late?'

'No. I . . . she and I don't . . . she's rather formidable. I didn't want her to feel I was making a fuss. But then I fell asleep over my book . . .'

'Ah. You were here reading last night.'

'Yes. I – I have a little job in a florist's shop called The Flower Bower; I worked there until five thirty, then came home and cooked myself some chicken and rice. Later I watched television, but it was boring, so I got out my library book. I took it up to bed with a cup of Ovaltine.'

'Was anyone else here with you at any point in the evening?'

'No.'

'And did you go out at all once you'd come home from the florist's?'

'No.' Her shoulders drooped. She looked at him wearily, sadly, like a dog taken for too long a walk.

Montgomery stood up. 'Thank you for your time, Mrs McPherson. Ros here will stay with you while we make some further enquiries.'

Margaret Kendall proved to be much more voluble. 'I can't believe it,' she said. 'What you've just told me seems com-

34

pletely unreal. I heard about the fire an hour ago from my newsagent. And about . . . the dead person . . . but I never *dreamt* it would be Robert! I thought it would be whoever had started the fire. I was just wondering whether to ring Robert at home when you arrived . . .'

Margaret's house was a comfortable little semi-detached, festooned with fading photographs of elderly people. Only on the tiled mantelpiece was there a bright, modern print depicting a laughing couple standing on a beach with two children.

'That must be your sister,' said Sergeant Bird, noting the facial similarities: deep-set eyes the colour of lead, a longish nose and strong, almost masculine jaw. Margaret was either older or more careworn, he decided. Her cheeks had that faint look of slackness, her hair was stippled with grey.

'Yes: she lives in Australia now. They emigrated twelve years ago, and have a wonderful life in Perth. I stayed here with our parents. Mother had suffered from a slight stroke and couldn't use her right arm properly. She needed help with my father, who had Parkinson's disease. In the event, Mother had another stroke three years later which killed her, so it was just Father and me until he died two years ago.'

'Have you managed to see your sister during that time?'

Margaret gave a small, bleak smile. 'She came here once during an extended European holiday while Father was still alive, but I haven't been able to get to Perth. I don't have the funds.'

Sergeant Bird nodded, and Montgomery took over the questions. 'Tell me about your employment at Furlong End Pharmacy,' he said. 'I understand you've worked there for several years.'

'That's right. It's been nine years, ever since Robert took over the pharmacy. I went in one day as a customer and saw his advertisement for staff in the window. At the time I was only doing a few hours in a local dress shop; I needed full-time work. We got on immediately, and I pride myself that a strong sense of trust developed between us over the years.'

35

'You were privy to the general ups and downs of running a business?'

'Oh, yes. He discussed everything with me. I was often able to make suggestions, from the "perfume of the month" promotions to broader strategies.'

'He must have regarded you as a very valuable employee.'

'He did.' There was harsh emphasis in her statement; briefly her mouth quivered.

'Was the business struggling in any way?'

'I . . . yes. Yes, it was. Robert did his best, but forces outside his control made the last few years one long attrition. First, the local supermarket opened up an in-store pharmacy . . . I don't know how they were allowed to do it. There are supposed to be rules against leap-frogging.'

'Leap-frogging?'

'Opening up a pharmacy between an existing pharmacy and the GP practice which they serve. But the distances didn't quite qualify, or something. Then there was all the reorganization of the local hospitals. Supplying their needs became a matter of hawking short contracts around to the lowest bidder. Just recently we lost an important contract with Grange Hospital.'

'Was Robert depressed about these events?'

'Well, naturally. But we were soldiering on, and hoping to find new business.' Her eyelids flickered. 'Are you suggesting . . . ?'

'What, Miss Kendall?'

'Well, that Robert . . . that he . . . I don't know.'

'Tell me how you view the events of last night.'

'I have simply no idea.'

'Why might Robert have been in the pharmacy at such a late hour?'

'Extra bookkeeping, perhaps. Stocks, invoices.'

'He has a linked computer at his home. Wouldn't that have been a more comfortable place to work?'

'He might have needed to check items physically in the store room. Or it could have been because of Theresa. He always did his best to avoid causing her concern.'

'Surely she knew that the business was at risk?'

'I don't think so. He tended to protect her from any unpleasantness. When a junkie was yelling threats in the shop just a couple of weeks ago, Robert specifically asked that Theresa shouldn't get to hear of it.'

Montgomery's interest cranked up a gear. 'Threats? Can you elaborate, Miss Kendall?'

'It was a thin, pasty youth of about twenty-four. We'd never seen him before. He wanted us to dispense a script for Diconal, a controlled drug, but we were on the alert for stolen forms at the time, and this one was a clear forgery. We stalled him, and called the police; he was arrested just as he was trying to run away.'

'What name did he give?'

'On the script it was Terence Bloom, but he told the police officer he was Sean Turner.'

'Sean Turner.' Montgomery caught the discreet movement of William Bird's pen as he noted this detail. 'Did he shout abuse at all the staff, or was it aimed at a particular individual?'

'He seemed to direct his venom towards Robert. He insulted him, then said something like: "You think you're so clever, but I'll get you." '

'Did he specify in any way?'

'No.'

'What about the arresting officers – did they give their names?'

'I – er, I can't remember. But one was well-built and walked with a kind of roll, and chewed gum.'

'Rennie,' said Sergeant Bird drily. Jackson's bosom pal seemed to mould his image on that of Louisiana policemen in 'road' films.

'That's it. PC Rennie. But what happened to the boy? Isn't he in custody?'

'That would depend on any previous convictions.'

'So you think it's possible that . . . that he set fire to the pharmacy as an act of revenge, unaware that someone was inside?'

'We're keeping an open mind at this stage, Miss Kendall. Is

there anyone else who could be described as nursing a grudge against Robert?'

'Andrew, I suppose. But if he is, he's no right to.'

Montgomery recalled the name. According to Theresa McPherson, this was the assistant who had 'had to leave' two months before. He had assumed that the departure was at Andrew's own instigation: there had been no suggestion from Theresa of any hostility . . .

'Andrew?' he prompted.

'I'm sorry. Andrew Dunster. He was Robert's pharmacy assistant for about five years. He was ordinary enough, a steady, quiet worker. It was quite a shock to me when Robert sacked him just a few weeks ago. Apparently he'd been stealing from the till, on more than one occasion.'

'Did he voice any threats?'

'No, he just slunk away. I didn't know what had happened until afterwards.'

'From what you saw of his character, could you envisage Andrew lighting fires as an act of spite?'

'I – not really. He was stolid and rather sullen. There's something *energetic* about creating fires, don't you think? But still – they say it's the quiet ones who surprise you.'

'Mm. I suppose you've already answered my next question, but – could you imagine Andrew committing a direct act of violence against another person?'

'I can only give an opinion.'

'That's all I'm asking.'

'I would say, only in a situation where there was no danger to himself.'

'Thank you. Have you any idea where Andrew is now?'

'He used to come into work from Gedling. I never knew his exact address. We think he still works somewhere on this side of Nottingham: Judy saw him driving a van along Parkdale Road the other day. We joked to Robert that Andrew's new employer must be a trusting sort to take him without references, but I'm afraid he wasn't amused.'

'And Judy is the assistant who has replaced Andrew?'

38

'Yes. She wants a proper career in pharmacy herself, so she was spending some time with us for the experience. Judy's filling in a year: she missed her A-level maths last summer because of flu, but she passed it in November. This autumn she'll be off to university.'

'I don't suppose there was any bad blood between Judy and Robert?'

'Goodness, no! Judy's a nice young girl, very open, quite engaging. Robert enjoyed teaching her the practicalities of the dispensary. They got on very well, almost like an uncle and his niece.'

Montgomery glanced narrowly at Margaret. He thought he could detect a faintly patronizing edge to her praise, but there was no answering reflection in her face. 'Was Judy present when the drug addict made his threats?'

'Yes, she was.'

'Can you tell me where we can contact her?'

'I can give you her parents' telephone number, but I'm afraid Judy herself won't be there just yet. She told me yesterday that she would be driving to Skegness today to visit her brother and his family.'

'Ah, well . . . we'll take the number, if you'd be so kind.'

'What do you reckon, Will?'

Sergeant Bird wriggled himself into the car seat. 'Margaret Kendall? One of those ladies who's had no choice in life but to be competent and fight her own battles. Tough on the outside, and probably well capable of the necessary professional façade in the shop, but inside – who knows? Soft, I doubt. Embittered? Maybe – but that's more likely to be directed at her family than her employer.'

'Just a reliable witness, then.'

'It would seem so.'

'That's my feeling so far. And she excels in that role, too: she's just provided us with no fewer than two prime suspects!'

5

Honour McPherson was tall and thin, with a stiffness of carriage compounded of dignity and incipient arthritis. Her duck-egg blue twin set matched highlights in her subtly hued silk blouse, and a lambent row of pearls softened the harsh lines of her neck. Even her spectacles looked expensive. Her eyes, though diminished in size behind the thick glass, were nevertheless sharp with intelligence.

If she was grieving, there was very little sign of it. Indeed, her companion, an altogether plumper and less tidy woman who had been introduced almost as an afterthought as Vera Blenkinsop, was much nearer to visible distress. She hovered close to Honour, glancing periodically at her face as if gearing herself to leap forward with succour in the unlikely event of a sudden noisy disintegration.

'Are you sure you won't let me call the doctor, dear?' she twittered, orbiting restlessly as Honour led the two detectives into a gracious drawing-room.

Robert's mother skewered her with a sharp glance. 'Vera . . . I've never favoured your calling me "dear" before; why on earth should I start now?'

'I just thought . . .'

'No doctor, thank you, but I'm sure these two gentlemen would like a cup of tea, if you'd be so kind.'

'Of course.' Vera lumbered from the room as Honour allocated seats with an elegant bejewelled hand. Beyond the brocade-curtained window, evening sun bathed the long garden with mellow light. Sergeant Bird had noted the generously proportioned grounds with approval when they arrived. This large stone house could well be a former rectory, he thought; behind the sycamore border a slender spire pierced the clear evening sky. It wasn't Southwell Minster; that majes-

40

tic edifice was two miles away in the direction they had travelled . . .

'We're sorry to intrude at this time,' began Montgomery.

She cut him off with a decisive gesture. 'You have your job to do. It must be just as unpleasant for you.'

'You were aware of the news . . . did Theresa contact you?'

A faint ripple of contempt crossed her immaculately made-up features. 'No. It was a young policewoman, a Miss Winger. She rang me at Theresa's behest . . . Tell me, Inspector, are you quite sure that Robert is dead?'

'As sure as we can be at this stage. He's been missing since yesterday, and a watch was found on the body which Theresa identified. It was engraved with a twenty-first birthday greeting from your husband and yourself.'

'I thank God that Alistair has been spared this. As you may know, he died of a heart attack six months ago.'

'Was he retired?'

'No – still working as a solicitor. He wanted to retire, but –'

Her jaw snapped shut. She looked impatiently towards the door to the hall, then back at Montgomery. 'What happened at the pharmacy?' she demanded. 'Why do you think there was a fire?'

'We're investigating many avenues at present,' said Montgomery carefully. 'There isn't enough information yet to make a judgement.'

'But it's ridiculous. Why was he trapped? Why couldn't he get away? *Why was he there at all?*'

'We're hoping you might be able to shed some light on that, Mrs McPherson. Theresa had been under the impression that he was here with you last night.'

A rattle of crockery heralded the advent of the tea-tray. 'I managed to find everything,' gasped Vera. 'These sponge fancies were in a tin; I thought it would be all right to bring them.'

'Perfect, Vera. Thank you very much.' Stiffly Honour poured tea for both the detectives, handed a cup to her friend and took one herself. 'Robert *was* here. He came for luncheon

41

and stayed for part of the afternoon. But then he left. I've no idea where he spent the evening.'

'Can you outline his stay more precisely?'

'If it helps. He arrived at one thirty, after the pharmacy had closed. We ate salad together in the dining-room, and discussed general topics: the church, my bridge evening, a trip of his to Newstead Abbey. The usual pleasantries. Then he offered to sort out some more of my husband's effects. These days I'm unable to climb into the attic, so periodically Robert would bring down trunks of clothes for charity, or boxes of papers to check through. I told him I would go out for an hour: it was my turn to arrange the church flowers.'

'I was there,' interjected Vera eagerly. 'We came back together, and Robert was just leaving. It was twenty-past four . . .' Gimlet eyes swivelled in her direction, and she faltered to a halt.

'Yes, Robert was leaving. He said he had things to deal with.'

'Had you expected him to stay for dinner?'

'We hadn't made an arrangement, but I was intending to ask him.'

'Were you surprised he left when he did?'

'I didn't give the timing any particular thought. It was not unreasonable; Robert had his own life to lead.'

'Where was he when you last saw him?'

'In the front doorway.'

'And what was his manner?'

'A little preoccupied, perhaps.'

'Can you remember his exact words?'

'No, but I can give you the gist. He thanked me for luncheon, said he had to go, and told me that he'd found Alistair's hacking jacket and hung it in the green bedroom.'

Under the guise of eating a sponge fancy (delicious!), Sergeant Bird watched the interplay of expressions on Vera Blenkinsop's face. Clearly she would have liked to contribute more to the conversation, but dared not. Instead, he spoke himself. 'Did Robert take anything away with him?'

'Just the briefcase he came with. Nothing else that I'm aware of.'

Montgomery took a sip of tea. 'Did Robert ever discuss with you any difficulties with the Furlong End pharmacy?'

Honour paused to return her own cup and saucer to the tray, then addressed Vera with a charming smile. 'Thank you *so* much for preparing the tea for us. I mustn't keep you from your home any longer. It's been so kind of you to come and sit with me.'

'But –'

'*So* kind. Let me walk down the hall with you. No, stay, Inspector: have another cup. I shall only be a minute.' Regally she escorted her friend to the front door, amid babbling protests about doctors and sedatives.

'I'm sorry,' said Montgomery when Honour returned. 'I thought Vera was an intimate of the family.'

'She aspires to be: the two things are not synonymous.'

'Were you aware that Robert was having financial problems with the business?'

'I had some suspicions, but he never admitted this outright.'

'So presumably he didn't ask you or his father for a loan?'

Her smile this time was purely mechanical, a mirthless baring of the teeth. 'Alistair could have lent him nothing. You see all this?' She made a wide gesture with her hand, encompassing the ornate ceiling, the room with its heavy furniture, the basking garden beyond. 'In a few months' time it will be converted into a nursing home for elderly people, and I shall be living in one small corner of it. It's the best I can manage. I wonder if Vera will be so keen then.'

'It was a rectory?' asked Sergeant Bird.

'That is correct. It was Alistair's family home, and quite run down when I first came to live here. But my husband was a very successful solicitor, so over the years we were able to restore the property and lavish care on each room. We developed the grounds, too; like the smallest cottage garden, the land here is both a piece of history and a living entity. Every bush, every shrub represents some memory of our married

43

life.' Briefly her narrow lips clamped together, as if to push back pain. 'Then last year, Alistair discovered that his partner had been embezzling from the practice; he had even stolen bond certificates left with them by clients for safe keeping. Alistair was an honourable man, Inspector. He made good with our own personal assets, and wrecked his health in the process. I keep up appearances, but essentially I have nothing now. Our home was mortgaged . . . the charity who are buying the property will take over that burden.'

'Robert knew of this?'

'Oh, yes. He knew we couldn't have lent him money even if we'd wanted to.'

'I see,' said Montgomery. 'Well . . . as you can imagine, we have a lot of investigations to carry out with respect to Robert's death, so we'll leave you for now. Once again, I offer my condolences. Is there anyone you would like us to contact?'

'Thank you, no. I am quite capable of making difficult telephone calls myself.'

She escorted them through the hall, where beneath an elaborately moulded ceiling three portraits hung in a row. The frame to the right enclosed a full-length painting of Honour herself, youthful but just as stern. Her blonde hair was piled high, and her bare shoulders gleamed above a strapless pale lilac evening gown. In the centre a tall, dark, intense young man with a moustache posed in jodhpurs and hacking jacket, a crop held lightly against his thigh. On the left was a slender young woman with raven-black hair, also attired for riding. Though she smiled vivaciously, the detectives could still discern a similarity of feature between this girl and the solemn man.

'Alistair?' murmured Sergeant Bird encouragingly.

'Yes, that is Alistair – before his hair went grey virtually overnight. And there is Isabel.' Her tone, which had warmed at the sight of her husband, remained soft as she transferred her gaze to the spirited beauty at his side. 'She was Alistair's sister.'

'Was?'

'She died at the age of twenty-four, doing what she loved best: riding. She was with the Belvoir Hunt – not that one is encouraged to admit such a thing these days. Her horse fell, and she broke her neck. They brought her back here in a Land Rover . . .' Visibly she rallied herself. 'I doubt I shall be allowed to keep these pictures in the hall. When the time comes I shall have them rehung in my rooms.'

Montgomery spoke quietly. 'Have you any sisters or brothers, Mrs McPherson?'

She shook her head. 'Robert was my last living relative, apart from some very distant cousins. Everyone I knew is gone. But don't look so concerned, Inspector. Now that I've lost all I had to lose, the fear of loss must also die. Nothing else can happen to me now.'

The acrid smell of old smoke still hung over the ruins of Furlong End Pharmacy when Montgomery and his sergeant approached the following morning. The weather was cool and a faint drizzle was beginning to fall; Montgomery pulled his raincoat tightly around him.

'Fire investigation,' he murmured. 'Poking among blackened beams and dead ashes. I can think of few activities more guaranteed to deepen the Monday morning doldrums except, perhaps, what Frobisher is up to right now.'

'Look at it this way, sir: Mondays are a write-off anyway, so we may as well get the least salubrious parts of the job out of the way and avoid jiggering up the rest of the week – don't you think?'

Montgomery snorted. 'It's as well one of us has constructive philosophies.' Yes, Will could be relied on to see the proverbial glass as half full. But Montgomery himself was finding it difficult to take a positive attitude. This place depressed him. Here, in a few searing minutes, not one life but many had been damaged beyond repair.

A man who had been squatting by the rubble straightened

up and hailed them. It was Jim Willoughby, a Fire Investigations Officer they knew well.

'How is it going, Jim?' asked Montgomery.

'Well, you know there have been difficulties because the roof and first floor collapsed. That's why it took a while to find the body . . . But we've done some clearing, and we're pretty sure there were at least two sources of ignition – one in the ground-floor back storeroom and one on the first floor itself. The agent downstairs at least was probably paraffin.'

'The body was found yesterday in the dispensary area near the remains of a couch.'

'Yes . . . from information we've been given, that couch was in the first-floor rest room. It must have crashed through when the floor collapsed.'

'So the body might also have come down from the first floor?'

'It's quite possible.'

'What about doors and windows?'

'Downstairs we can say with certainty that everything was locked, but upstairs . . . it's impossible to tell now. A window *could* have been open.'

Montgomery knew that the store room had extended a few feet out at the back as a single storey. Whoever lit the fires could therefore have had an easy escape route over the flat roof. If the arsonist on this occasion was Robert himself, why had he ended up trapped? Had the flames flared too suddenly? Had his clothes ignited?

That long crack in the skull of the charred corpse still needed explaining: Ian May had been unable to rule out external violence. Supposing, then, an intruder had been involved, someone looking for drugs, perhaps, who hadn't expected the pharmacist to be present so late in the evening. Say he had panicked and lashed out, killing Robert McPherson, then tried to obliterate all signs of the deed by destroying the shop . . . all very possible, but how did he gain entry in the first place?

A key was essential . . . which drew attention inevitably towards Robert's past and present employees. There would be security codes and procedures, of course, but Robert wouldn't have been the only person privy to these: in case of illness or delay, his assistants would have been allowed to open up the shop to sell items such as general toiletries. Supposing the sacked employee Andrew Dunster had a duplicate key and had returned to the pharmacy on Saturday night intent on theft or vandalism? Perhaps his act of revenge had turned out to be more lethal than he had expected.

There was a third alternative: Robert may have willingly opened the door to his assailant. Perhaps that person was someone he knew and trusted. There might even have been an appointment, or an assignation . . .

Once more Montgomery felt the damp chill of the unseasonal weather. Shoving his hands into the deep pockets of his raincoat, he followed Willoughby round the side of the ruined building to the small concrete-paved compound at the rear. A four-year-old Ford Fiesta was parked there, its blue paint blistered and discoloured.

'Smythe did the checks you asked for yesterday,' said William Bird. 'That *is* Robert McPherson's car. We've directed the people making house-to-house enquiries to include it in their questions. Someone may have seen the car arrive, or noticed another vehicle parking behind the shop.'

Montgomery peered inside. 'Make sure there's a full forensic examination,' he enjoined. 'Especially the boot. We can't rule out the possibility that this Fiesta has carried inflammable substances.'

William Bird raised his eyebrows. 'You think so?'

'Frankly, I don't know. But my mind is staying open until I have the evidence to close it. Let's hope that Frobisher can assist us there . . . Thank you, Jim. I look forward to your report.'

'Next stop, the mortuary,' murmured Sergeant Bird.

Frobisher was just finishing his examination. He nodded at the two detectives, then peeled off his gloves with a flourish and strode over to the ante-room.

47

'There's no sign of carbon in the air passages,' he told them as he sat down and stretched out his long thin legs. 'None in the stomach, either. I'm confident he was dead before the fire got to him.'

'Cause of death?' enquired Montgomery.

Frobisher tilted his chin down to stare over his half-moon glasses. 'You've seen the body. Externally there's very little to go on. The soft tissues were too badly damaged. He may well have simply died from inhaling poisonous fumes, like carbon monoxide or cyanide. I've taken blood from the deep vessels for the usual tests. If drugs or alcohol were involved, we'll find out that, too.'

'I was wondering about the skull fracture.'

'Ah, that. There was a heat haematoma just beneath. A collection of brown, foaming blood – I'll show you in a minute.'

'Does that mean the fire was the cause?'

'Yes. The blood literally boils out of the venous sinuses and the skull bones themselves, and accumulates in the extradural space.'

'So he wasn't whacked on the head?'

'It's most unlikely.'

6

'Judy's up in her room. I'll fetch her for you.'

Mrs Pearce, in the manner of many exemplary citizens, looked faintly apprehensive as Montgomery and Sergeant Bird introduced themselves. She half turned as if to climb the stairs, then veered back to face them once more.

'I'm sorry – come in here. It's not very tidy, I'm afraid.' Portions of newspaper were scattered over the beige living-room sofa; rapidly she gathered them together. 'We weren't sure – that is, we didn't know if anyone would be wanting

Judy. She only started work at the pharmacy seven weeks ago. We're all very shocked by what's happened.'

She disappeared, and the detectives looked about them. The house was a large 1930s semi-detached with a 'lived-in' feel, full of cheerful family artefacts. Books, videos and a box of chocolate mints were stacked on the coffee table. In the corner, a glass display case gleamed with sporting awards: cups and medals and ribbons.

A languid tortoiseshell cat was monopolizing one of the armchairs; as William Bird moved forward to stroke it, a boy of about fourteen craned his head round the door, peered at them curiously then vanished with a muttered 'Sorry'.

Moments later a girl some four or five years older entered the room. Judy Pearce was an attractive, athletic-looking teenager, with steady blue eyes and thick, glossy blonde hair tied back in a pony-tail. She wore a long-sleeved T-shirt with red and yellow stripes, tight black trousers and ankle boots. With more confidence than her mother had shown, she introduced herself and invited them to sit down.

'I'm glad you've come,' she said. 'Ever since I heard the news, I've been wanting to talk to someone about Robert and the shop . . . Mum doesn't know, but I was going to contact you myself.'

'You have some information for us?'

'Well . . . not exactly. But I saw something potentially suspicious, and I feel so guilty now that I didn't take it seriously at the time.'

'Go on.'

'It was a gang of about eight teenage boys. They were peering into the shop on Saturday night when I drove past at quarter-past nine. There was a light on in the dispensary: I did wonder if Robert was working late. I wasn't quite sure what to do, so I drove past again. The second time they'd wandered off down the precinct, so I went home.'

'Did you recognize any of these boys?'

'They looked like a gang I'd seen before, loitering odd afternoons in the precinct. I've also seen them hanging around the car-park up the road. The eldest boy looks about sixteen, but there's a young fair-haired boy who tags on who can't be more than fourteen.' She paused. 'Do you know Margaret Kendall? She told me the fair boy was a neighbour of hers called Glenn. She asked me to keep an eye open if he came into the shop because she thought he might be tempted to shoplift.'

'Was Glenn there on Saturday night?'

'I'm fairly sure, yes.'

'Did you see any of the youths carrying weapons?'

'No.'

'What about petrol cans, or bottles of any kind?'

Judy shook her head vigorously. 'Nothing like that! If I'd thought they were going to start a fire, I would have rung somebody!'

'And presumably you didn't witness any attempt to break in?'

'True. I thought the pharmacy was perfectly safe. Apart from the steel grille at the front, the doors have coded locks and special alarms. I believe they're linked to your headquarters.'

'That is correct. Now, Judy, can you recall if Robert actually said he would be working late that night?'

'He didn't say.'

'Did he mention *any* of his plans for Saturday evening?'

'No. I was with him in the morning, but we just got on with the work. I remember telling him I would be going to Skegness on the Sunday, but he didn't reciprocate. He just wished me a pleasant day . . .'

'Had he mentioned appointments, or meetings, in any kind of context?'

'No. Unless . . .' She frowned. 'I don't know whether this is significant, but he had some peculiar phone calls two or three weeks ago. A man with a sort of cockney accent rang the shop and asked for Mr McPherson, so I passed him on to Robert. They didn't talk for long, though. Robert said he wasn't interested in whatever the man was proposing. I thought it was a pushy drugs rep – some of them just won't take no for an answer. When he rang again a few days later, Robert was really abrupt with him, which is unusual because he was normally very courteous.

'Last week – I think it was Tuesday – I was in the dispensary while Robert was up in the rest room. Margaret had asked me to chivvy one of our cosmetics suppliers whose delivery was overdue, and I picked up the phone with half of my mind on the details of our order. I heard a voice, and realized that Robert must have rung out from the extension upstairs. The voice wasn't his, though: it was the cockney man again.

'Five minutes later I popped upstairs to ask him to supervise an over-the-counter sale of Codis. Legally you have to do that because Margaret and I aren't qualified. He was just finishing his conversation. I heard him say, "Ten o'clock, then," before he put the phone down.'

'Ten o'clock,' repeated Montgomery.

Her candid blue eyes met his. 'Yes. Naturally, I assumed that was a daytime appointment, but now . . . well, who can say?'

'*Were* there any 10 a.m. appointments during last week?' asked Sergeant Bird.

'I don't think so. Not specifically. Let me think . . . Someone came in to sell us fruit teas, but – no, that was midday.'

'Did Robert seem upset by these phone calls?'

'A bit, perhaps. It's hard to be sure. I always felt he hid his feelings to a large extent at work.'

'What was his character as you saw it?'

'He was quiet and diligent, civil to customers, even the awkward ones. He wasn't a chatterer. If one of us made a joke he would respond politely, even chuckle sometimes, but he didn't initiate any himself. He took every opportunity to teach me about the medicines because he knew I was going to study pharmacy properly myself. I've got a place at university this autumn.'

'Where's that, Judy?'

51

'Here in Nottingham. I can continue living at home.'

'Well done. So Robert helped you, and was generally quiet by nature. Did you get any feeling that he was depressed?'

'Not especially.'

'And Saturday morning was the last time you saw him?'

'Er, yes.' Her gaze slid away to the floor. 'I can't believe he's dead. Everything seemed quite normal in the shop. Margaret must be devastated – and his wife, of course . . .'

'Yes, it's been a shock for everyone,' agreed Montgomery. 'We won't take up any more of your time just now, Judy, but we may need to ask further questions at some future date, or require you to make a statement. Thank you for your help today.' He stood up and wandered to the display case by the wall. 'Are these your cups?'

'Some of them are mine – tennis trophies from school, and athletics medals. But those medals on the left are Roger's.'

'Is that the brother in Skegness?'

'No – my younger brother. He lives here with us.'

While Montgomery and Judy were talking, Sergeant Bird had risen to his feet, stroked the soft warm fur of the nearby tortoiseshell cat and circumnavigated the room in a surprisingly noiseless manner for a man of his bulk. The door to the hall was open a crack; with a cat-like alacrity of his own, he suddenly swung it wide. There, inches away in a frozen attitude of concentration, crouched the youth who had stared at them earlier. As his cover vanished, he jumped in alarm. 'Er – I just wondered if you wanted tea,' he croaked.

'Thank you, but we're just leaving. It's Roger, isn't it?'

'Yeah.'

Montgomery strode to join them. 'We were admiring your medals. Are they all for soccer?'

'Yeah.'

'Which national team do you support?'

'Forest.'

'Of course. Well, thanks again, Judy. Oh . . . just one more thing. On Saturday night, did you notice Robert's blue Fiesta parked in the courtyard behind the shop?'

'I'm sorry; I didn't look.'
'Fair enough. We'll be on our way.'

'I wouldn't want to get Glenn into trouble.'

Margaret Kendall seemed quite disturbed by the detectives' second visit. 'He didn't actually steal anything in the shop – I made sure of that. But you say Judy saw him outside the pharmacy on Saturday night?'

'Yes. We were wondering if you could let us have his address.'

'He lives in this road. Five doors down to the left – number 45. But, Inspector . . . Glenn is basically a good boy. You can take my word for it. I'm sure he wouldn't have destroyed the pharmacy. He knew I worked there, and I've been a friend of his mother's for years . . .'

'Sometimes young lads get carried away by peer pressure. One can never be sure. But there's no evidence against him as yet. We just want a chat with him.'

'Is he . . . your main lead?'

'As yet we're still gathering information.'

Her look of distress deepened. 'Glenn is an only child,' she said. 'He wasn't spoilt, though, just rather solitary. He'd try to join in games with the three brothers from number 49, but they rarely let him because he wasn't as fast and physical as they were. He used to read a lot of books. Lately, Kathleen tells me it's been video games . . . If he's been involved in anything criminal, it won't have been his idea. Please treat him kindly.'

'Hello, Glenn,' said Sergeant Bird as an adolescent boy opened the door of number 45 and squinted at them suspiciously. 'I'm Detective Sergeant Bird, and this is Detective Inspector Montgomery. Is your mother at home?'

'Why do you want her?' His voice was only partially broken. He had a studious face and light brown hair. His jeans and white cotton T-shirt were clean and conservative; only the bright scarlet necktie he wore struck an incongruously raffish note.

'We need some help with an investigation we're making, and we'd like a little chat with you, if you don't mind. Your mother will –'

'I've done nothing wrong,' he squeaked.

'No one is saying you have. We'd just like your assistance – ah, is it Mrs Foley?'

Introductions were effected, and soon the four were seated in the pleasant living-room, Kathleen Foley eyeing her son with unhappy speculation.

'You know about the fire in Furlong End Pharmacy?' said Sergeant Bird quietly to both the Foleys. 'It's only half a mile away from here.'

'It's a tragedy,' said Kathleen Foley. 'Margaret has worked there for years. Her boss died in the fire.'

'We heard that you were in the area on Saturday night, Glenn. We hoped you might have seen or heard something that would help us.'

Mrs Foley held up her hand. 'Wait,' she said. 'You've got the wrong boy. Glenn was at St Felix's youth club.'

'Is that true, Glenn?'

The boy's eyes flickered evasively, but he said nothing.

'What time did he arrive home, Mrs Foley?'

'Just before eleven. He was later than he promised. We said half-past ten, didn't we, Glenn?'

'There was a snooker competition,' he murmured.

'Look at me,' she said firmly. 'You were supposed to be with Roger Pearce at the youth club. Now you know how easily I can check. *Were* you there?'

A blush spread from his chin to the tips of his ears. 'No,' he said after several seconds of silence. 'I didn't want to go. Youth club's boring.'

'Were you in the precinct near the pharmacy?' asked Sergeant Bird.

Glenn nodded.

'Tell me who was with you.' Slowly he persuaded the reluctant boy to divulge the names of his companions, a process not helped by Mrs Foley's expressions of outrage.

'They're none of them his usual friends,' she insisted.

'What did you all do at the precinct?'

'Just hung around – you know.'

'Did you see anything out of the ordinary going on at the pharmacy?'

'A light was shining inside. There wasn't normally one after hours . . .' Glenn winced as he realized his error. Luckily this time his mother forbore to interrupt, but her increased respiratory rate left them in no doubt that she would have words for Glenn later on.

'Anything else, Glenn?'

The boy gave a dispirited shrug. 'No.'

'Did you or any of the other boys try to get inside?'

'No.'

'Did anyone have any paraffin or petrol?'

'No.'

'How about matches?'

'Some of the guys smoke.'

'Did you notice any cars in the vicinity of the pharmacy?'

'Yes. A blue Fiesta parked at the back. You could see it from the road.'

'What time was this?'

'Nine, ten . . . It was there while we were.'

'And how about people? Did you see anyone at all entering the pharmacy?'

'No. We were at the other end of the precinct a lot of the time. But I saw the chemist coming out.'

Sergeant Bird felt himself staring. 'The pharmacist? You saw Mr McPherson?'

'Yes. He left the shop at ten thirty, just a few minutes before I went home. He came out of the access drive up the side of the shop and walked away up the road . . . He must have gone back in again, though, mustn't he?'

William Bird didn't know what to say.

55

7

Montgomery and his sergeant met up again in the station corridor the following morning.

'I've been mulling over yesterday's interviews,' said Montgomery as they headed towards the CID room, 'and a few things don't quite make sense.'

'The car,' replied William Bird instantly. 'If Glenn saw it that night, why didn't Judy?'

'That was one of the points. Judy says she noticed the light in the dispensary at nine fifteen and wondered if Robert was working late. A natural progression from that idea would be to look for his car. Even allowing for the distraction of the gang of youths, she had a good chance of spotting it from the road – remember, she drove past not once, but twice, and the second time the boys had moved on. As we know, the Fiesta wasn't hidden behind the building. It was at the far end of the access drive, and would have been partially illuminated by the pharmacy side wall security light.

'So why did Judy miss the Fiesta? Either it wasn't there at that point, or she genuinely didn't see it – or she was misleading us for some reason. Normally I'd find that hard to credit: she seemed a particularly frank young woman. But there's another thing – why didn't she tell us that her brother Roger knew Glenn?'

'Oh, I think that's understandable, sir. She was probably protecting him from a police grilling. And Glenn did insist to us that Roger was nothing to do with the gang. Or she may not even have known. A career-minded girl of nineteen can't be expected to keep track of all her adolescent brother's friends.'

'True, Will . . . come on through.' They passed through the spacious room shared by the junior detectives, and entered

Montgomery's own glassed-in office. A potted *Pilea* on the windowsill was beginning to shrivel and droop; Sergeant Bird itched to water it. 'There was something else,' went on Montgomery. 'Something I can't quite put my finger on. It was Judy's manner . . . it seemed to change when I asked about her last sighting of Robert. She stopped looking at me; there was something odd, something hesitant about her . . .'

'I noticed that, too, sir. It's hard to assess the significance, though.'

'At least we can check on the Fiesta when we get the results of the house-to-house enquiries. And Glenn – what do you think about him? Do you reckon he's a reliable witness?'

'He volunteered the facts readily enough: seeing the car, and seeing Robert McPherson leaving the pharmacy. As you established yesterday, he knew McPherson well enough by sight, him being a local retailer.' He pursed his lips. 'I think Glenn would only have lied if he'd had any involvement with the fire – and in that circumstance I would have expected him to have been much more afraid of us than he was.'

'Mm. So . . . let's say Glenn told nothing but the truth. He and his cronies hung around the precinct from about eight thirty. At nine fifteen they wandered up to the pharmacy end because the failing light outside made them notice that the dispensary inside was illuminated. They peered through the window but didn't see anybody in the main shop; the interior of the dispensary itself was only partially visible. They then went to buy beefburgers from On the Hoof, a small fast-food establishment on the main road four hundred yards away, then ambled back towards the precinct. They stopped outside the Fox and Grapes pub, smoking cigarettes and hoping to meet a group of girls who sometimes came that way on a Saturday night. The girls didn't turn up, so the boys headed back to the precinct around a quarter to ten. Exciting evening, don't you think? At half-past ten Glenn spotted Robert McPherson emerging from the pharmacy's side access drive and walking away up the road. He didn't notice whether the dispensary light was still on. A few minutes later he realized he'd have to sprint home, so he left the rest of the gang where they were.'

Montgomery gave a small shrug. 'Maybe Robert himself went off for something to eat, though he was cutting things a bit fine in that locality at half-past ten. We'd better check when the PM report comes through – see what they say about stomach contents.'

A faint frown bisected Sergeant Bird's forehead. 'That's the wrong direction, sir. If you go east along Furlong End Road from the precinct, all you come to are houses – and the car-park.'

'The car-park . . .' Montgomery looked thoughtful for a moment, then shook his head. 'The fire is supposed to have started between eleven and twelve. As Glenn said, Robert must have gone back inside.' He roused himself visibly. 'We need all Robert's movements, everything we can get between that last sighting by his mother and the arrival of the fire brigade. We need to track down Sean Turner and Andrew Dunster.'

'Sean Turner will have a custody record downstairs. Rennie was the arresting officer if you want a full description.'

'I'll put Brian on to that. He's Rennie's pal. Andrew Dunster might be a bit more tricky to find. All the pharmacy records were destroyed with the building. There might be something on Robert's personal computer at home, but I'm loath to bother Theresa again so soon . . . Margaret Kendall mentioned Gedling. Brian can begin with the phone book.' He grimaced. 'In the meantime, someone else has the jolly task of tracing seven teenage boys!'

It was late afternoon when Frobisher rang. Sergeant Bird was at his desk, attacking computer keys with his usual deliberate, pile-driving force, when movement behind the glass panes in Montgomery's office caused him to glance upwards. Montgomery emerged through the doorway, his lean face stunned.

'There's a new development in the McPherson case,' he

announced to the handful of his team who were present. 'I've just received some curious toxicology results from Professor Frobisher.' He waited as Graham Smythe jettisoned a report he was studying and lifted an eager face. 'It seems that Robert McPherson was killed by a cocktail of anaesthetic drugs!'

If Jackson had been at his station, he would have emitted a stagey whistle. At the desk adjoining his empty one, Smythe sat round-eyed.

'How bizarre,' murmured Sergeant Bird.

'Yes,' said Montgomery. 'The drugs in question were . . .' He consulted a slip of paper in his hand. ' . . . thiopentone sodium and vecuronium bromide.'

'That's the poison they use for blowpipe darts in South America, isn't it?' said Smythe. 'The Indians in the jungle.'

'One of the more refined forms, yes. I'm told there are a whole group of drugs derived from curare which anaesthetists use to relax the muscles of patients. It makes surgery easier.'

'What about thio . . . thio-whatever-it-was?' asked Grange, a beefy detective constable.

'Apparently that's given first to render the patient unconscious. Then gases are administered to maintain that state. Otherwise, you've got someone on the operating table who is completely paralysed but can feel every cut.'

'It happens,' said William Bird darkly.

'Yes – and the hospital gets comprehensively sued.' Montgomery paused, still dazed by the revelation. 'I think I'll have a chat with Ian May about this. We need to know a few more details . . .' He left them excitedly discussing the implications of the news, and telephoned the young GP-cum-police surgeon.

'You mean McPherson? The body in the pharmacy?' The doctor was interested, but sounded less impressed than Montgomery's junior colleagues.

'Yes.'

'Must have been suicide, then. Poor chap.'

'Why do you say that?'

'Well . . . a pharmacist would know the properties of these drugs. It's a foolproof and relatively painless way of killing yourself, not dissimilar to the lethal injections they give judicially in America. Presumably there were stocks of these drugs on the premises.'

'We'll check on that, of course. But, Ian . . .' Montgomery was not entirely convinced by the pat scenario. That heat haematoma – might it have masked a blow to the head after all? Frobisher hadn't ruled this out completely. And where did the fire itself fit in? He couldn't ignore the fact that at least two individuals harboured a strong grudge against McPherson. 'Do the drugs have to be injected? Is there any other way?'

'No. They only work intravenously.'

'Then . . . how could he have given himself both drugs without the first one taking effect and rendering him unable to continue?'

There was a faint snort at the other end of the line. 'Nothing to stop him mixing the two in the same syringe. Thiopentone takes a few seconds to work – long enough to squirt the whole lot into a vein. The total volume would be less than 20ml.'

'I see. Thanks for that. Sorry to have disturbed your evening surgery.'

'You're welcome. It's all hay fever and holiday vaccinations at present. Keep me posted, won't you, Richard?'

'You can rely on it. I might need to pick your brains again.'

Montgomery's colleagues were still in the throes of lively discussion when he returned to their office.

'We're puzzled about the fire, sir,' said William Bird. 'If our pyromaniac targeted the pharmacy and Robert McPherson was trapped inside and died, then how come he was full of anaesthetic drugs? And if it was suicide, why the fire? We reckon this has to be murder, but the method seems unduly elaborate . . .

'Supposing after Glenn had gone home that group of boys

did break into the pharmacy. McPherson may have surprised them, and been knocked on the head for his pains. They may have panicked then, especially if he'd recognized them, and decided to kill him . . . But how did they know to use those particular drugs? Why didn't they just cosh him again? Squeamishness? Hardly. It doesn't make sense.'

'No . . .' To Montgomery, the feel was one of calculation, not panic. Someone who knew their pharmacology had injected McPherson with those drugs. So who were the possible candidates? Margaret Kendall might not have professional qualifications, but over nine years she would have imbibed plenty of relevant knowledge. And all manner of useful books would be to hand . . . Likewise, Judy Pearce and her predecessor, the sticky-fingered Andrew Dunster. And what about Sean Turner, the Diconal addict? He had fraudulently tried to obtain tablets, but he could well be adept at the injection of other substances. In all these cases, firesetting was the next logical step, to deflect the blame and hopefully disguise the murder method employed . . .

Montgomery's chain of thought remained incomplete as Jackson strode heavily into the room. 'Nice to see you all sitting comfortably on your arses,' he said. 'Some of us have spent the day grafting.' He turned to Montgomery. 'You wanted leads on Andrew Dunster and Sean Turner. Well, I've got news. They used to be in the same class at school. They drink in the same pub. And for the last two months, they've worked together.

'They're both employees of a man called Geoff Crabbe.'

8

Montgomery determinedly tried to concentrate on his book. Beside him in the bed Carole lay asleep, a featureless mound, only the raven-black crown of her head visible against the pillow. He could hear her soft, regular breathing and the distant whirr as the fridge motor clicked on in the kitchen below.

On the printed page of *Lord of the Flies* the stranded boys had begun to organize themselves in the absence of adults. There were two definite factions, but they were co-operating and their behaviour was reasonably civilized – so far. True to life, the fat boy 'Piggy', with his glasses and asthma, was treated disparagingly by the other children, but this had little connection with the desert island. Even the hero, Ralph, displayed the same casual cruelty towards his lieutenant . . .

Montgomery sighed, and inserted his bookmark. It was no good – ideas about the Furlong End case intruded insistently, inviting him to theorize despite the inadequate data. Geoff Crabbe . . . cockney accent. Could it possibly have been Crabbe whom Judy had heard on the telephone making a mysterious ten o'clock appointment? Andrew Dunster formed an undeniable link between Crabbe and the pharmacy. But plenty of people other than Crabbe carried their cockney accents away from the East End of London. The caller could well have been a 'pushy drugs rep', as Judy had suggested. Then again, the matter which so irritated Robert McPherson may have been neither medical nor pharmaceutical. They simply didn't know at this stage. Tomorrow there would hopefully be much more information.

Turning out his bedside light, Montgomery burrowed down among the warm sheets and closed his eyes. The image of Crabbe, brash and superficially plausible, danced behind the lids and refused to disperse. In Montgomery's estimation he had always been a minor villain, lightweight, not one of the sinister thugs you might expect to commit murder. But it was some years since Montgomery had had dealings with Crabbe. Who knew what company he might have been keeping in the meantime? The criminal face of Britain was changing, hardening . . . And Crabbe was a coward. Perhaps if he had felt his interests were sufficiently threatened, he had disposed of the source of that threat . . .

But Ian May had confidently pronounced the death as suicide. He had said the two anaesthetic drugs were a sensible choice to bring about that end. And Robert McPherson *had* been under pressure . . . his business was failing, and his father had recently died. Montgomery suspected that the relationship between Robert and his mother had been a cool and distant one. Filial duty . . .

Slowly he stretched his limbs and assumed a new position. There was definitely a need to uncover much more about Robert McPherson's character and past history. Had he ever been clinically depressed? Was he taking any medication?

When Montgomery finally slid into sleep, however, his dreams were not of Robert McPherson. Instead, he saw a lush tropical island with a boy swimming in a green lagoon. Another boy, this one fat with glasses, hesitated nearby, saying, ' "I can't swim. I wasn't allowed. My asthma –" '

' "Sucks to your ass-mar!" ' retorted the first boy. The voice was juvenile, unbroken, but as he waded out of the water he turned his head. With a shock Montgomery saw the pointed teeth and flashing rings of Geoff Crabbe.

'Let's see Margaret Kendall first,' said Montgomery to Sergeant Bird the next morning. 'She's the person most likely to know whether anaesthetic drugs were stocked at the pharmacy, and she may be able to give us more background on Robert McPherson's general state of mind in recent weeks. She claims to have been something of a confidante.'

'I'd have thought hospital pharmacies were more likely places to find vecuronium,' mused Sergeant Bird as they climbed into a police Metro.

'We'll find out . . .' Montgomery took the wheel; he quite enjoyed driving, and sometimes found William Bird's pace too sedate. When they reached 35 Fielding Avenue, no one answered the front door bell. 'Out shopping, I suppose, or maybe visiting Judy . . .'

An elderly woman making a painful progress along the

63

pavement turned into the next-door front garden. She fumbled for her key, then spoke to them over the wall. 'If it's Miss Kendall you want, she's gone to work.'

Montgomery exchanged glances with William Bird. This neighbour clearly had yet to hear about the tragedy.

'Green Triangle Pharmacy,' she went on. 'Can I give her a message for you?'

'Er – no, thank you.'

'That was quick work,' growled Sergeant Bird as they cruised down the road towards Furlong End Pharmacy's nearest rival after the supermarket.

'Indeed.' Montgomery pulled on the handbrake, climbed out of the car and stared at the pharmacy's generous frontage. He entered the light, roomy interior, passed the well-stocked shelves and stated his business to the middle-aged man behind the counter.

The man nodded gravely. 'It's ironic,' he said. 'We'd been trying to head-hunt Margaret for months, but she wouldn't leave Furlong End. I like loyalty. What happened up there is dreadful – none of us envisaged her coming under these circumstances. It'll take her a long time to get over this . . . I'll just go and fetch her.'

Montgomery pocketed his warrant card and waited. When Margaret Kendall appeared, she gave a shamefaced little smile and motioned them into a small comfortable alcove labelled 'Patients' Consultation Area'.

'I know what you're thinking,' she said at once. 'But I had to work. I was going mad at home. They said I could start as soon as I liked – and I've got to pay my way. I don't have any other source of income.'

'They wanted you particularly, I gather.'

'Yes; I think it's my knowledge of all the local customers . . . I can't get over the facilities they have here. This alcove for private discussions, for instance – Robert would have killed for this!' She started; blood flared into her cheeks, and she bit her lip. Smoothly Montgomery introduced the subject of medicine stocks.

64

'Were any anaesthetic drugs ever kept at Furlong End?' he asked.

She gave him a puzzled look. 'Well . . . yes. We had a contract to supply Grange Hospital with all its theatre requisites – until recently, that is. We just lost it and were lumbered with a lot of stock.'

'I don't understand,' said Sergeant Bird. 'I thought Furlong End served the general community, not hospitals.'

'Ah, that's how things used to be. Now it's a commercial free-for-all, part of the new "purchaser/provider" ethos.'

'Were drugs such as thiopentone still on the premises?' interjected Montgomery.

'Yes.'

'And vecuronium bromide?'

'Yes. May I ask why . . . ?'

'You'll appreciate our need for circumspection just at present. We're still investigating on many parallel fronts. But we haven't yet ruled out the possibility that Robert was depressed and took his own life. You said before that he told you everything. Were you just referring to the business problems, or did he ever divulge anything personal?'

'He did once,' she said, her gaze losing focus. 'The first year I worked for him we had a bottle of Christmas wine after closing the shop, and it loosened his tongue. He started talking about childhood Christmases, and then summers in that house near Southwell where Honour still lives. Despite everything he said about presents, a sense of isolation permeated his story – the gaping distance between his parents and himself.'

'He was an only child, I believe.'

'Yes. He had a favourite aunt, though, who was young and lots of fun. Isabel used to play with Robert, and show him her own childhood toys. Apparently there was a cedar wood summer house she loved at the bottom of the garden, where they'd spend whole afternoons together. Robert was devastated when she died. It was a hunting accident – ah, you know about this? Her mount clipped a wall and she fell and broke her neck. Robert ran out of the house just as they were unloading her body from the Land Rover. Imagine the trauma for a little boy!'

'Did Robert tell you all this?'

'In outline. I must confess I looked up an old news report for the year in question. There was a photograph of Isabel – she looked so spirited and beautiful. It was all terribly sad. Later, Honour touched on the subject, too . . . Robert invited me for tea at the house. He wasn't married then, he was still living at home. I admired the portraits in the hall, and we got talking about Isabel. Then I noticed that a lot of her personal effects were on display about the house: dolls, books, a tea set. We went into the garden – it's beautiful, so long . . . I was hoping to see the summer house, but it wasn't there any more. They said it had burned down two or three years after Isabel died, and they didn't have the heart to rebuild it. I think someone was careless with a garden rubbish fire.'

She twisted her fingers together. 'Inspector, I can't help feeling that Isabel's death affected Robert's parents' attitude towards him. Because of their own grief, they couldn't give him attention just when he most needed it. They all grew cool and formal with one another. When I was there, I felt no warmth between him and Honour.'

'Have you visited since?'

'No. I don't think Honour liked me very much. Her revelations were brief; most of the time she was dry and high-handed. I suspect she thought it unsuitable for Robert to be offering tea to his pharmacy assistant. Goodness knows what she thought when he married Theresa.'

Montgomery saw his chance to steer the conversation back to the present. 'How do they get on now?' he asked.

'Who?'

'Honour and her daughter-in-law.'

'I haven't seen them together myself, but I know Robert usually visited Honour alone, even for dinners and Sunday lunches.'

'How about Robert and Theresa? Do you think all was well between them?'

Margaret Kendall hesitated; Montgomery thought he could sense an inner struggle. 'Yes,' she said at last. 'Theresa is very mild-mannered, never raises her voice, can cook and keep the house well . . . Robert had all he needed on the domestic front. There was no reason for friction there.' She looked as if she would dearly have loved to say more, but clamped her lips together and stared levelly at Montgomery.

He felt he was close to something useful, but what? 'Perhaps she was less able to share the business worries than the people on the spot – like yourself,' he said casually.

She seized on his gambit like a wasp gouging into jam. 'Yes!' she hissed. 'Theresa was nowhere close to Robert's intellectual level. Sometimes she would come into the shop to see him, and she would ask him – such simple questions. Things that a child might want to know. It seemed to me that he protected her from the nuts and bolts of life, from forms and calculations, accounts and anxieties. He let her drift in her world of flowers.'

'Theresa is very pretty,' put in Sergeant Bird, nodding benignly.

Margaret Kendall went puce. 'Mm,' was all she could say.

'And young. I would say she's still in her twenties.'

'She's thirty-one!'

'Ah,' said Montgomery. 'Well, we appreciate the time you've given us. I've just one more question . . . We're still trying to clarify the events of Saturday night. You live quite close to Furlong End Pharmacy. Did you happen to pass the precinct yourself at any time that night?'

'I'm afraid not. I would have said.'

'May I ask how you spent the evening?'

She shrugged. 'If it helps. There was a church bazaar coming up, and my friend Emily was running the white elephant stall. I went round to her home to help sort through the donated items and price them, and she asked me to stay on for dinner, which I did. I suppose I must have left about nine o'clock.'

Sergeant Bird's pen was poised. 'Her full name?'

'Emily Middleton.'

'And she lives . . . ?'

'In Jarrett Street. Number 24.'

'Thank you. Did you come home directly from there?'

'I, er . . .' Her gaze fell. 'I popped into the off-licence on the corner of Arnold Street for a bottle of sherry. I treat myself to the odd glass on Sundays.'

'Did you see any sign of Glenn Foley while you were out in the streets?'

'No. I'm sorry.'

'Right. Well, thanks again. And please thank your new employer for us. We'll let you know as soon as we have some hard news . . .' They left the shop.

'We'd better see Theresa next,' said Sergeant Bird as Montgomery eased the Metro away from the kerb. 'Margaret Kendall's no fool; she must have twigged the significance of our enquiries about thiopentone *et al*. I doubt she'll keep it to herself.'

'She's not close to Theresa, as we ascertained, but I agree some third party might be eager to blab the news. Very well, then – Theresa.'

The neat modern house was deserted, its diamond-paned windows gleaming softly in the sunshine. The two detectives headed for The Flower Bower, and minutes later were being ushered into a cool back room with an overpowering scent of petals and moss.

Theresa was winding creamy lilies into an elaborate funeral wreath. She stared at her visitors uncomprehendingly as Montgomery gently informed her of the pathologist's latest finding.

'I don't understand,' she said after a long pause. 'I don't know what you're saying. Robert had *drugs* in him?'

68

'Yes. We can't say at this stage whether or not they were self-administered, but they are drugs known to bring about a painless death.'

Theresa backed against a two-foot cross of red and white roses, her face twisted in bewilderment. 'He wouldn't have left me,' she whispered. 'I know he wouldn't.' She gave a strangled sob, then her pale blue eyes flicked back towards Montgomery. 'Was there a needle in his arm?'

'I'm afraid I don't know all the forensic details.'

'There must have been, mustn't there, if he did it himself? And Professor Frobisher would have seen it. So, you see, he can't have killed himself.'

'We're having to keep our minds open at the moment.' Montgomery strolled to the bench. 'Theresa – did your husband ever mention having trouble with a man called Geoff Crabbe?' Almost subliminally he heard her intake of breath; fleetingly her face registered despair.

'Geoff Crabbe?' she faltered when the silence was becoming unendurable. 'I don't think so. Why?'

'Or a man called Sean Turner?' Montgomery ignored her question.

'No.' Now she couldn't meet their gaze at all. Her cheeks, even her lips were pale.

'Did Robert receive any threats that you know about?'

'I – I'm sorry; I can't think straight.' Her knees began to sag and Sergeant Bird half lifted her to the nearest chair.

Montgomery watched, his compassion laced with uneasiness. 'We didn't mean to distress you,' he said. 'We'll come back another time. But we felt you had a right to know the details of Robert's death.'

Her eyes brimmed; fluid quivered and glistened as her lower lashes bent under the weight. Then suddenly there were runnels, ever-accelerating rivulets of brine snaking down her face to drip from her chin and splash to the floor.

The detectives walked towards the flimsy bead curtain which separated the back room from the shop. From the other side they could hear the murmur of voices.

'Anaesthetic drugs, you said.' This voice was Theresa's. Montgomery paused with his colleague and half turned. 'Painless death,' she went on in a rasping whisper. 'Nothing to do with the fire.'

'The fire didn't kill him,' stated Montgomery.

'Thank you.'

He nodded and stepped through the curtain. Theresa's employer, a tall hook-nosed woman, was just pressing change into the palm of a customer. She sent him an interrogatory glance, and he paused for a few words of acknowledgement. Behind him Sergeant Bird negotiated the lightly jangling curtain and looped it to one side in the position it had occupied on their arrival.

Some instinct made Montgomery look back. There among the wreaths and the heavy funeral-parlour fragrance stood Theresa, her head flung back, her teeth clenched in a rictus of torment. Her writhing hands gripped the broken stems of a bunch of lilies, while scattered all around her lay the shredded remnants of their petals.

9

'Theresa did have a point about the needle,' commented Sergeant Bird as the Metro purred along the pleasant winding road to Southwell. The hedgerows were still bursting with spring flowers, while up in the sky a languid sun rolled out hazy heat.

Montgomery sent him a cool glance. 'Is that meant to be some kind of kindergarten pun?' he enquired.

'Not exactly intended . . . it just happened. But she's right. No needle was found at the PM. And anyone injecting themselves with those particular drugs would have lost consciousness before they could dispose of the needle somewhere else.'

Montgomery was less impressed. 'I don't know,' he said. 'You saw the body, Will: it was savagely charred. The needle could have dropped out or become unrecognizable.'

'The legs were in the worst state,' argued Sergeant Bird, 'but the arms weren't too bad. Remember the metal of his watch and glasses survived.'

Montgomery sighed. 'True. All right – we'll ask Frobisher to have another look. He may have already done so when the toxicology result came through.' He stared out through the windscreen as they crested a hill and the double spires of Southwell Minster shimmered in the middle distance, silvery sentinels above the mellow ochre stonework. The news had affected Theresa profoundly; now they had the demanding task of facing her mother-in-law.

Detective Sergeant Jackson scowled up at the red-roofed barn. Pub bar rumours had narrowed down the search to this semi-rural location, and he had expected to find at least some human activity here, if not the specific men they were seeking. As it was, the main door was locked, and the wooden plaque beside it stating 'Morgifts Ltd.' unhelpful.

Smythe emerged from the corner of the building. 'There's a window round the side,' he said. 'I can see a desk and lots of papers – some sort of office. This could be the right place.'

Jackson gave a non-committal sniff. It was twelve forty-five, and he was hungry. 'Pity Crabbe's home is ex-directory,' he said. 'Since he doesn't trade under his own name, we don't know whether this is his outfit, or not. If it is, I reckon they're having a lunch break. They're probably down the pub – which isn't a bad idea.'

He waited while Smythe circumnavigated the barn once more, rooting and craning.

'There's an answerphone flashing,' he said on his return. 'Shall we wait, or . . . ?'

'Let's come back in an hour,' said Jackson.

Montgomery steered the car through the narrow streets of Southwell, past the red-brick cottages with their pantile roofs and the famous sixteenth-century coaching inn towards the elegant Prebends with their mainly eighteenth-century architectural styles. The Minster glided past on the right, its towering angles softened by a rim of horse chestnut and copper beech trees. Soon Southwell was behind them, and they were once more in rolling countryside. The village sign for Bramton appeared; Montgomery turned left past the tiny grey church where Honour McPherson worshipped and prepared to pull up outside her house.

'She's got a visitor,' warned Sergeant Bird, spotting Honour's tall figure standing at the gate while a much shorter man spoke with her earnestly. 'He's wearing a dog collar.'

'We'll go past and wait.' Montgomery smoothly accelerated and turned left again into a cul-de-sac of more modest houses and bungalows, all russet dwellings constructed from local brick. Half-way down he parked and switched off the engine. 'Just to recap,' he said, 'we'll be asking her if Robert had any history of depression, if he was taking –'

'*Yoo-hoo!*'

'Who on earth . . . ?' Montgomery was startled.

'It's Vera Blenkinsop. That garden over there. It's us she wants, I'm sorry to say.'

Vera left the garden and bustled towards them. 'I thought it was you,' she beamed. 'I hope you didn't mind me shouting like that – I thought you might start up the car and go away again. Did you come to see Honour?'

'We'll be calling on her shortly, yes.'

'I've just been round there myself. The rector's with her. She looks terrible today – as if it's all just sunk in. Would you like to come to my house for a few minutes?'

'Well, that's very kind, but –'

She lowered her voice. 'There are some things I think you ought to know.'

'In that case, thank you.'

They followed Vera past a white-painted front gate into the garden of a small 1930s double-fronted bungalow. The flower beds were overstocked with blowzy, unkempt blooms. Crushed behind banks of marguerites and Michaelmas daisies, delphiniums and lupins leaned at crazy angles, while at ground level an undulant wave of lobelia and campanula surged out over the narrow pathway.

Just a weekend, thought Sergeant Bird. One weekend with secateurs, a fork and some canes, and one could make real inroads into this.

'You like gardens, Sergeant?' Vera beamed at him.

'I do indeed.'

'Then you must come round the back.'

Even in his eagerness to see the flowers (tempered with some trepidation as to their state) William Bird noticed how much more assertive Vera was in the absence of Honour. Was there a Mr Blenkinsop? he wondered.

The rear garden was mainly laid to lawn, but the south-facing border held a kaleidoscopic mix of shrubs and herbaceous plants. Vivid red-hot pokers burst out of the maelstrom, and unpruned fuchsia bushes erupted like fountains of blood-drops at random intervals.

He paused by a spray of golden broom.

'Ah – you like broom. So do I. I try to learn the Latin names – that one's *Cystitis*.'

Behind her broad shoulders, Montgomery pulled an incredulous face. William Bird struggled to keep his own within sober limits.

'Come and see my scabies,' she invited.

Now Montgomery had fallen behind most markedly. Sergeant Bird doggedly kept his own steps in time with Vera's waddling ones, and soon they reached the expected clump of candytuft-like flowers. These were a double flowering variety in an attractive shade of mauve. 'Scabious,' he murmured, nodding his approval. '*Scabiosa caucasica*.'

A wood pigeon cooed from a distant tree. The air was still,

and very hot. As they walked on slowly down the garden, the border came to a straggly end; ahead lay a small clutch of fruit trees, and beyond that a neglected area of uncut grass.

They stood between two plum trees and now the light pattern was dappled, the air cooler. To the left, Sergeant Bird saw that the character of the boundary had changed. The wall behind the mixed border had been scarcely four feet high, allowing glimpses of the next-door garden and neighbourly chats if one so desired. This end portion, however, seemed different, somehow darker. Closer inspection showed him that the wall here was a foot higher, and behind it reared a variety of tall bushes, raising the total barrier to nine feet. He recognized an orange *Berberis*, flanked by a row of hollies. Only the lilac at the farthest end had leaves one could grasp without thick gloves.

'It was my husband Alec who did most of our gardening,' explained Vera. 'He died three years ago, and I haven't really kept up with it since. I was always better at cakes and jam . . .'

Montgomery came to join them. He glanced around at this more shadowy end of the garden and absently rubbed his upper arms before taking charge of Vera. 'You said you had some information for us,' he put to her.

'Yes. I was just about to . . . I thought you'd want to see . . . Well, we'd better go inside.'

The interior of the bungalow was as shambolic as the garden. 'Best not to be overheard,' she said, motioning them towards an overstuffed chintz sofa. 'Honour would probably rather you didn't talk to me at all. But she didn't really describe Robert's demeanour to you adequately, and it could be important.'

'Last Saturday?'

'Yes. He was just leaving the house as Honour and I came back from the church. She started to ask him if he wanted to stay for supper and he was *abrupt* with her, quite rude. I'd never seen anything like it before. He was normally so courteous and deferential . . . He said he had things to do, and when she tried to delay him, he became very agitated. He was worried, Inspector. There were things on his mind.'

'Is this what you wanted us to know, Mrs Blenkinsop?'

'Part of it . . . I think I might have some idea what was upsetting him. I, er, I hesitate to *insinuate*, but . . .'

'Go on.'

'Well . . . it's Robert's wife, Theresa. I've only met her twice, but she's a pretty girl and one can easily remember her features.'

'What about Theresa?'

'I saw her three weeks ago in a tea-shop in the city. She was with a man who wasn't Robert. They were laughing, and their manner was . . . most *familiar*.'

'Do you know this man?'

'No.'

'Can you describe him?'

'I'm not sure . . . He had light brown hair and a slim build – quite similar to Robert's, really. But it wasn't Robert. Definitely not. I saw the face. Let me see . . . his clothes were bright, very modern . . .'

'What sort of age was he?'

'Forty, perhaps. Older than Theresa.'

Sergeant Bird leaned forward. 'Could it simply have been a friend, or a relative?'

'No. He kissed her hand twice, and *lingered* both times.'

'You're suggesting it was a lover,' said Montgomery.

'I am, yes.'

'Even if that was the case, have you any reason to think Robert knew?'

'Well . . . not directly. You see, I was in the tea-shop with Mary Wilsmore, a friend from the WI. She knows Honour and Robert, too. Now, I've heard that she went round to The Old Rectory last Saturday while Honour and I were doing the church flowers. She says she rang the bell and no one answered, but we know Robert was there. What if she's not quite telling the truth? She's a bit of a gossip, is Mary. What if she said something to him about Theresa? That could have sent him over the edge.'

'What do you mean, over the edge?'

'Well, you know . . . the tragedies in that family.' Her eyes were beginning to gleam. 'He's just lost his father, and of course there was Bella – you do know about Bella, don't you?'

Isabel . . . 'Yes,' said Montgomery. 'Robert was very young then.'

She nodded. 'He lost his memory. It affected them all for life, though. Especially Alistair. And now Robert himself has died in a fire. Don't you think there's a pattern?'

A build-up of tragedies, and betrayal by the only person whose love had seemed unqualified . . . perhaps. Vera Blenkinsop was in unwitting agreement with Ian May. But this information about Theresa was thin. Laughter and kisses in a Nottingham tea-shop. It was hardly damning. Unless . . .

Something teased at the back of Montgomery's mind, but evaporated before he could secure it. He looked at his watch, and stood up smoothly. 'Thank you for your time, Mrs Blenkinsop,' he said. 'We'll check on your information with all discretion. If you think of anything else, do let us know. We're still trying to fill in Robert's movements during the hours between his visit to Honour and the fire at Furlong End.'

She willingly agreed, and accompanied them to the front gate. 'Don't forget,' she warned, 'Honour is looking frail today.'

In this at least, Vera had not exaggerated. Age had suddenly caught up with Honour McPherson since the detectives had last seen her, as if this latest blow had finally eroded her every reserve of vitality.

'You have your job to do,' she said flatly when Montgomery apologized for bothering her.

'It's a lovely day,' said Sergeant Bird. 'Perhaps we can talk in the garden?'

'My colleague is particularly fond of well-kept gardens.'

76

Montgomery's urbane smile turned into a glower as soon as Honour's back was turned. 'What are you playing at, Will?' he hissed. 'This lady has arthritis!'

'Call it a whim, sir . . . but not an idle one.'

Montgomery rolled his eyes, and accompanied Honour in a slow progress round the side of the house to a rose garden, where she discussed the merits of 'Richmond', 'Peace' and 'Glenfiddich' for some minutes with William Bird. Then she moved on to an attractive circular herb garden where the individual varieties were separated by stone edging in a pattern resembling the spokes of a wheel.

'Your mint is so disciplined,' marvelled Sergeant Bird. 'Mine always spreads rampantly.'

'The secret is to keep the plants in individual flower pots. Sink them so that the rims are just covered with soil.'

'That would work for lemon balm as well – another gangster.'

She gave a reflex smile, an echo of graciousness, then sat neatly on an adjacent carved wooden bench. 'I enjoy talking about my garden,' she said, 'but you've come to ask more questions about Robert. Or perhaps to tell me some news?'

She scarcely moved as Montgomery described the forensic finding of anaesthetic drugs. Only her eyelids flickered behind the spectacles, and her mouth tightened. 'I see,' she said quietly when he had finished. 'Not an accident, then?'

'No. We need to know if Robert was depressed – if he'd ever talked about suicide.'

'He never said anything of that kind to me.'

'Had he ever received treatment for anxiety or depression? Tablets from his GP?'

'Not that I know of.'

'Was he ever a hospital patient?'

'Only for his appendix, when he was eleven. I'm sorry, Inspector, but I really can't help you.'

'What about his marriage? Was all well there?'

'To the best of my knowledge, yes. In fact, the last time I saw

77

him he mentioned an outing that he and Theresa had enjoyed only the previous Sunday.'

Again there was a flutter at the back of Montgomery's brain. This time he seized the idea and stored it away in a safer file. Meanwhile, Honour was looking at him intently. 'Inspector – can you tell me what you've found out so far? Am I allowed to know yet?' She swallowed. 'You say there were drugs in Robert's body – but there was also a fire. What do you think this means?'

Montgomery suspected that Honour McPherson would not be fobbed off lightly by tales of 'lines of enquiry'. 'We don't yet know,' he said. 'We've been investigating a series of suspicious fires in the area, which appear to be the work of a single arsonist. There are some similarities of method between the blaze at Furlong End and these other incidents, but also some differences. It's possible that the perpetrator *wanted* this fire to be attributed to the serial arsonist, when its true purpose was to cover the traces of a crime.'

'A crime . . .'

'Yes. We've been asking you about Robert's state of mind, but alternatively he may have been attacked on Saturday night, perhaps rendered unconscious with a blow and then drugged.'

Her lined face grew pale. 'You have a suspect?'

'We are checking the movements of people with a possible grudge against Robert.'

'I see.' She stood up abruptly for one so apparently frail. 'Please keep me informed,' she said with a spectral attempt at crisp command. 'I need to know these things.'

'Of course.'

'Thank you . . . Now, Sergeant, let us view the rest of the garden.'

Slowly they meandered through the spacious rear garden, from *Weigela* to silver birch, from lavender border to a hidden arbour with statues and a weathered stone seat. Towards the tall bushes at the rear boundary wall the quality of maintenance began to falter: the lawn was cobbled with moss and daisy clumps, and its grasses grew long.

Honour halted with a low cluck of irritation. 'I have a gardener twice a week,' she said, 'but he can't cope with all this. I find myself wondering how much the trustees of the nursing home will be prepared to maintain.'

She turned as if to retrace her steps, but Sergeant Bird had spotted a faint rectangular image in the grass just ahead, a lipping of the lawn over some long-buried foundation. 'Was that the summer house?' he asked curiously.

'No. It was an old greenhouse, a ruin even when Alistair and I were first married. We built the one you saw behind the herb garden . . .' Her brows drew together in a small frown. 'I don't recall mentioning the summer house to you . . . ?'

'A colleague of Robert's told us that it was burned down two or three years after Isabel's death.'

'That's true, and regrettably it was my fault. It was a molten day in July, and I exchanged my glasses for a pair of sunglasses, leaving my normal ones on a garden table. They must have been concentrating the light, because in the early afternoon a pile of bone-dry garden waste ignited nearby, and the flames spread to the summer house. It was all cedar wood; it couldn't be saved.' She shook her head, then gave him a wry smile. 'I fear you'll have to look further afield for your arsonist.'

William Bird acknowledged her weak attempt at levity with a smile of his own, and benignly scanned this distant, less immaculate end of the garden. 'It must have been fun for Robert to come here and play with his aunt away from the other grown-ups. Where was the actual site of the summer house? Near that magnolia?'

'No – even further up the garden. I'm afraid you can't see it now, because when Alistair became less capable of heavy work, we gave away a portion of our land to a neighbour whose garden abuts our own. They were keen to expand.'

'Something of a wrench, nevertheless?' murmured Montgomery, drawing near the twosome.

'Indeed.'

Honour looked tired and drawn; with compunction Montgomery escorted her back to the house and asked his own final question. 'Just one more thing,' he said as they stood in the fine hallway where the portraits glowed their witness to happier times. 'We have been informed that a neighbour of yours tried to gain entry here on Saturday while Robert was on the premises and you were out arranging the church flowers. She rang the bell, but no one responded. Is your bell faulty, by any chance?'

'I don't believe so.' Honour tested the device; it rang out clear and sharp. 'I dare say Robert was in the attic at the time, and couldn't hear.'

'Would you mind if we conduct a small trial?'

'Please do.'

Within minutes Montgomery was crouched in a large, well-filled attic, his lungs oppressed by the dust and the solid build-up of the day's heat beneath the roof. From far in the distance came three faint vibrations.

'Yes,' he said after scrambling down thankfully, 'Robert may well have failed to hear the bell.' He brushed a streak of dirt from the side of his trousers. 'Thank you for all your help,' he said to Honour.

'I'm sorry I couldn't tell you very much. But you *will* let me know of any new developments, won't you?' Her face kindled with a brief urgency before sagging back into the cruel ravines of age and deep grief.

'If there's definite news, you shall hear it,' promised Montgomery.

The Metro sped back towards Nottingham.

'Mary Wilsmore,' murmured William Bird, writing the name in his notebook. 'Either she was lying and did see Robert, or she never got into the house.'

'That's about the sum of it. Will – did you make any notes last time we came here?'

80

'A few, afterwards.'

'Could you check back for me, please? Have you anything on Robert's conversation while he was eating lunch with his mother on Saturday?'

'Let's see . . .' The sergeant pawed at the pages with his blunt fingers. ' "Lunch one thirty. Disc. church, bridge, trip to Newstead. No confidences re business finances . . ." '

Montgomery's lean cheeks were pulled even tauter with concentration. 'Newstead – I thought so. And Honour has just told us they went a week last Sunday. That's when *we* were there . . . and who did we run into but Geoff Crabbe? It's not his usual kind of haunt . . . Could it have been a rendezvous, I wonder?'

'But Theresa was with Robert.'

'Perhaps he left her in the tea-shop, or something . . . Or maybe . . .' Montgomery slowed the vehicle right down as an appalling idea struck him.

'Sir?'

'Nothing.' Smartly he accelerated away. 'No evidence yet . . . Tell me, Will, why were you so determined to see the whole of Honour's garden?'

'I wanted to check out a theory of mine. Last time we visited Honour I looked down her garden from the drawing-room windows and could just make out the end border. There was a splash of purple far on the left and some orange towards the middle. Well, today I saw those colours again – from Vera's garden. Remember that raised wall on the left at the bottom, where those neglected fruit trees were?'

'I certainly do. It was rather desolate, with all that long grass.'

'Rearing above the wall were various bushes of the spiteful variety, hollies and so on . . . In the middle I saw a *Berberis* in bloom – bright orange. And at the far right a lilac was spilling over . . . I was pretty sure that we were looking at the bottom of Honour's garden from the other side, and when we walked round to The Old Rectory I was able to confirm the orientation. The two gardens *do* abut, at right angles. And Honour's lilac and *Berberis* corresponded exactly in their positions to those we had just seen . . .'

'So?'

'So why grow such an impenetrable thicket? That border's about as friendly as an electrified fence.'

'Well, Honour said herself they'd given away some of their land when Alistair could no longer manage the work. She probably dreaded the prospect of Vera striding up through her back garden yelling "*Yoo-hoo!*" and made darn sure it couldn't happen!'

'You're probably right. And they –' He broke off as the signal of his pager filled the car. ' 'Scuse me, sir . . . may I borrow your mobile?'

The caller was a plaintive-sounding Jackson. 'Are you and the boss ever coming back?' he asked.

'We're on our way now.'

'Well, tell Montgomery we've got some big news here. Geoff Crabbe has disappeared. No one has seen him – not his staff, not his wife. He's been gone since Saturday.'

10

'Sean's got plenty of previous,' said Jackson an hour later. 'Possession, mainly, but right now he's on bail for that attempted prescription fraud.'

Montgomery gave a grunt of acknowledgement as Jackson jolted the car to a halt next to the tall brick barn. With Smythe to the rear they strode in through the open door and entered the office section.

'Sean Turner, Andrew Dunster,' Jackson identified the occupants. 'This is DI Montgomery.'

Turner was thin and pasty-looking, with untidy dark hair and deep-set black eyes. Dunster was fair-haired, pink-cheeked and altogether flabbier. Both stared sullenly at the three detectives.

'We've come to ask you some more about your employer,' began Montgomery.

'There's nothing to say,' sneered Sean. 'We haven't seen him. Sorry, and all that.'

'Has he ever disappeared before like this?'

'He goes abroad every now and then. Business trips.'

'Leaving you in charge?'

'That's right.'

'But he arranges it first, doesn't he? Squares it with you.'

'Usually, yeah.'

'Only usually?'

Sean Turner's venomous little eyes flickered away from Montgomery.

'Did he give you advance warning this time?'

'He's the boss. He can do what he likes.'

'Come on, Sean. His own wife doesn't know where he is. She's frantic with worry.'

Sean gave a non-committal shrug.

Montgomery strolled to a nearby filing cabinet. 'What exactly does Morgifts encompass? What's the nature of your business here?'

Sean Turner repeated the shrug. 'Mail order stuff,' he said carelessly. 'Mainly imported. Some we sell via existing catalogues, some we market ourselves with strategic ads.'

Montgomery could guess the implications of this – the flooding of national dailies with hyperbolical half-page advertisements, the competitive prices, the unredeemed shoddiness of the goods dispatched . . . It was safe enough to offer a refund guarantee; most people were too busy or too embarrassed to complain. All perfectly legal, then, and Crabbe's initial investment could be recouped tenfold . . .

Pigs might fly, thought Montgomery. Once a fence, always a fence. Morgifts was almost certainly a cover for other, even less savoury, activities. 'May we look around?' he asked.

'You got a warrant?'

'I could waste some magistrate's time if you like. But I thought you'd appreciate the opportunity to co-operate.'

'Look if you want.'

Montgomery addressed Andrew Dunster. 'Would you show these two officers round, please? Thank you.' As they left, he turned again to Sean. 'Listen,' he said. 'We want Geoff for questioning in connection with a case of suspicious death. It might be nothing to do with him – but it's odd that he should disappear just after the incident. If he *is* in trouble, you don't want to get dragged in as an accessory, do you?' Sean's own alibi, which centred on a Nottingham nightclub, was being verified.

The young man blinked, and from close range Montgomery saw how tight the pupils were in his narrow eyes. So he was still getting his supplies from somewhere . . .

'How long have you worked for Geoff?' he went on.

'Four or five years.'

'What do you do?'

'Driving, mainly; shifting supplies, packing . . . I cover for the office if no one else is around.'

'So Andrew does most of the paperwork?'

'Yeah. He hasn't been here long, though. A woman called Molly used to do it, but she moved south.'

'Was Andrew employed for any particular reason?'

Sean maintained an expression of disinterest. 'He was a mate of mine. I knew he was looking for a job, so I told Geoff.'

'What about his knowledge of pharmacy? Was that a useful credential?'

'I don't know what you're getting at.'

Montgomery sighed. 'Sean – remember what I said? We might be able to keep you out of this altogether.'

'If I don't know anything, Mr Montgomery, then I *am* out of it.'

'All right. Just tell me this. Where do *you* think Geoff is?'

'He's got a mistress. P'raps he's on holiday.'

'Do you know her name?'

'Barbara Leadbetter. She lives somewhere in Grantham.'

'Have you anything else for me, Sean? Anything about Andrew?'

'Best ask Andrew himself.' The telephone rang. ' 'Scuse me.' He turned his back with an insolent sneer. 'Hello, Morgifts . . .'

Andrew Dunster had almost completed his circuit of the barn. He passed an internal door and paused a few yards beyond. 'That's it,' he said chalkily. 'You've seen the lot.'

'What's behind that door?' demanded Jackson.

'I don't know. Geoff keeps the key.'

'You must have some idea.'

'I haven't.' His voice rose and wobbled.

Jackson stood closer, invading Dunster's personal space. 'What was Geoff's connection with Furlong End Pharmacy?'

'I – I don't know of any.'

'Then it's only you and Sean we have to worry about. The two people who held grudges against Robert McPherson.'

'I told you, I was at home on Saturday night, watching the telly with my sister.'

'We know that's what you *said* . . .'

'Check it out!'

'We are doing. But I'd expect your sister to cover for you . . .' He thrust out a truculent chin. 'Here's the scene from our side. McPherson fires you; Crabbe takes you on. Crabbe arranges a meeting in the pharmacy late on Saturday night; McPherson dies in a fire. Now, in my book, you're in it up to your neck. Why not do us all a favour and tell us what you know?'

Dunster's lips trembled and his pudgy cheeks gleamed with moisture; a wave of his sweat rose to their nostrils.

'This is a murder case,' Jackson reminded him.

'I don't know what happened – that's God's truth.' Dunster was gabbling now. 'Geoff took me on because he had some dodgy pharmaceuticals to flog, and Sean told him about me. Sean knew I had some dirt on McPherson, so he'd have to do whatever Geoff wanted. Geoff made an appointment for ten

85

o'clock Saturday night. That's it – that's all I know.' He spread his fleshy hands.

'When did you last see Crabbe?'

'Saturday morning, about eleven.'

'Mm.' Jackson nodded towards Smythe, who promptly scribbled a note on his pad.

'Where does Sean fit in? Why did he try to rip off some drugs from Furlong End Pharmacy?'

Andrew Dunster's babyish mouth curled in contempt. 'He's addicted to Dikes. So is Geoff.'

Smythe, who had momentarily lost concentration, looked up, startled. 'What – they watch girls rolling round together in blue movies?'

'Dikes, you dork. Not *dykes*.' Jackson gave an exaggerated sigh as Smythe remained bemused. 'Diconal tablets. Controlled drugs.' He turned back to Andrew. 'Go on.'

'Geoff gives Sean money to go to a particular supplier.' The exchange had been lost on Andrew. 'He doesn't, though. He tries to get them for free using stolen FP 10s. Pretends he's unemployed, on benefit. Then he pockets the cash himself. But he shouldn't have tried to hit Furlong End. Sean can be an arrogant bastard sometimes. Thinks he can get away with anything. Geoff was livid when he found out . . .'

Montgomery silently materialized from behind a stack of packing cases.

'Mr Dunster here is just about to find us a key to this room,' announced Jackson.

As the three detectives drove back to the station, Montgomery contemplated Crabbe's wife Monica, whom he knew of old. She would have to be questioned, but Jackson's particular brand of sensitivity was likely to prove counterproductive. The more calming presence of William Bird would be preferable.

'Well done with those pharmaceuticals,' he told Jackson. The locked room had been crammed with boxes of drugs, obscurely labelled, some stamped 'Bulgaria'.

'Why didn't Crabbe get his Diconal from the same place?' mused Smythe. 'Perhaps they don't manufacture them.'

'Or he wanted to be sure of the quality where his own hide was concerned,' said Montgomery drily. 'Tomorrow I'd like you to track down the mistress, but not actually interview her. Ditto any other friends and business associates of Crabbe you can manage. I shall take Will to see Monica Crabbe – she's met me before.'

Smythe leaned towards Jackson, who was driving. 'I'd appreciate it if you'd refrain from calling me a dork in front of suspects,' he said stiffly.

'You *were* a dork,' came the answer. 'And you didn't need me for the demonstration.'

Crabbe's home was a sprawling 1970s residence, over-embellished with wrought-iron and gilt. Everywhere gleamed carriage-lamps, looping terrace wall decoration, ornate gates.

Monica Crabbe opened the door to Montgomery hesitantly. 'It's you,' she said, and for a second he saw fear flare in the back of her eyes.

'Yes. May we come in?'

'If you've some news for me . . .' Nervously she twisted her fingers together, and the orange-painted nails seemed to flash little messages. She led them into a long room with a beige carpet and cream leather three-piece suite. The mantelpiece was cluttered with Capodimonte sculptures, and on the bureau opposite stood a florid reproduction Dentzel carousel clock. 'Do you know where Geoff is?' she asked when they were seated.

'You didn't report him missing,' said Montgomery.

'No . . .' Her gaze fell. She still had her perpetual tan, he noted, and the thick mascara and coral lipstick had been religiously applied, but for the first time since he had known her she looked middle-aged. Too many hours spent on sunbeds had affected her skin: her neck sagged; her cheeks held a hint of chamois leather.

'He's been away before,' she went on. 'Buying trips in Europe, various things . . . I didn't want to panic too soon. But now I'm rather frightened. It's been five days.'

They all knew that talk of buying trips was patent nonsense. Crabbe would have informed his wife in the normal way. That left two other options: either Monica suspected he was with a mistress (and surely Crabbe would have offered some cover story), or she believed he had been involved in a crime, perhaps one which had gone wrong . . .

'Why do *you* want him, Mr Montgomery?' she asked.

'Didn't Sergeant Jackson tell you when he telephoned?'

'He just said Geoff was wanted for some enquiries. But he's going straight now, honestly he is. He runs an import business, and he's doing very well. Look . . .' She lifted a hand to indicate the room and its decorations. More faulty logic, thought Montgomery; much of their material wealth was almost certainly the proceeds of crime.

'We do want to ask Geoff some questions, about a serious incident last Saturday. But you haven't told us yet why you didn't report him missing.'

'I – I don't know.'

'Did he ever mention Furlong End Pharmacy to you?'

'No.'

'You're sure he said nothing about an appointment there?'

'No.'

'When did you last see him, Monica?'

'Saturday lunch time.'

'And what did he say then?'

'He was going to play golf, and he said he'd be late home. I assumed he would be having dinner with friends from the club.'

Sergeant Bird took details of these friends, then asked, 'Have you got a recent photograph of Geoff?'

She rooted in an album and detached two pictures, one a head and shoulders view of her husband, the other a full-length print of him sitting on a beach. On both he was smirking cheerfully. 'Is he in trouble?' she whispered.

'We don't know,' said Montgomery. 'We're trying to find out.' He steepled his fingers. 'Monica – I'm sorry to ask you this, but did Geoff have any special female friends?'

'You mean a mistress?' Her lips tightened, and her face became bleak. 'I might as well tell you; you'll find out anyway. Yes, he did. Somewhere there's a woman ten years younger than I am who's been getting the prime of my husband and none of the responsibilities. I don't know her name, and I don't want to know.'

'Why do you put up with it?' he asked softly.

Again her gaze flickered around the room and its contents, although this time her hands were clenched and still. It was answer enough.

'May we look around?' asked Montgomery.

She nodded, and led the way into the dining-room. Here were more expensive artefacts, including an attractive porcelain tea service which could have passed for Meissen. Montgomery was reminded of the dainty little cup found in the ruins of the pharmacy. Strenuous efforts to remove the soot had revealed it to be white with a pink rose pattern; across the bottom were the words 'English Bone China', plus a number and a motif incorporating the letters TP and a Staffordshire knot. He had described these details to Carole, who had a keen amateur interest in antiques, but disappointingly she had assessed its vintage as mid-to-late twentieth century on the basis that registration numbers beginning with a nine were only recorded from 1962. She had promised to try to find out more. Meanwhile, the pharmacy staff had denied all knowledge of the cup. He would wait for additional data before asking Monica or anyone else . . .

For the next ten minutes they toured the sumptuous interior, including a conservatory extension which housed an inviting turquoise swimming pool. There was no sign of Geoff Crabbe.

Montgomery paused in a glacier-white bedroom with mock Doric columns and a plethora of gilt mirrors. 'Are any of his clothes missing?' he asked.

'No,' she said, pulling open the doors of a tall fitted wardrobe so that they could see inside. 'I've already checked.'

'What about holdalls or suitcases?'

'They're all here.'

'Do you have a caravan?' asked Sergeant Bird. 'Or a boat, perhaps?'

'No. We were thinking about a caravan, but – no.'

Delicately Montgomery broached the subject of Geoff Crabbe's Diconal addiction, but Monica was angry and defensive, denying all knowledge.

On the doorstep, Sergeant Bird spoke again. 'Let us know if you hear anything of Geoff, won't you? And we'll do the same.' He smiled, and she nodded jerkily, casting an injured look towards Montgomery.

'You drive,' said Montgomery as they reached the car. He pondered the evidence of the morning, chin on chest, while William Bird made a stately progress towards the city centre. There was a sick, heavy feeling in his stomach which had started two days earlier and worsened as the information built up from various quarters. Now a conclusion loomed which was almost too awful to contemplate.

'Will . . .' he said at last.

'Yes?'

'About Geoff Crabbe . . .' He took the photographs from his pocket and studied the leering face. 'Have you been thinking what I've been thinking?'

'Two missing men, one charred body? Yes.'

'We've no real proof that that body *was* Robert McPherson. None at all.' His jaw tightened as he lifted his eyes and stared unseeingly through the windscreen. 'What if it was Geoff Crabbe?'

11

'Let's recap,' said Montgomery when they reached his office. 'The body at Furlong End was identified as Robert McPherson because it was found inside his locked pharmacy, wearing the remains of a pair of spectacles and a watch engraved with McPherson's name. At that time, only McPherson was known to be missing.

'But none of that "proof" is irrefutable, is it? The goalposts have moved . . . we need biological evidence of identity – teeth, blood, something . . .'

Sergeant Bird absently patted the pocket where his pipe had once lived. 'Frobisher managed to get blood for those carbon monoxide and drugs tests,' he said. 'He extracted it from one of the deep vessels which was still intact. We could ask him to take some more.'

'Yes, but we need something to match against the sample: blood or tissue taken ante-mortem that we *know* was from Robert McPherson. If he hasn't been ill recently, then such specimens are unlikely to exist. The only other way of matching would be by taking blood from relatives.'

'Like they did with the Romanovs?'

'Broadly. They needed several subjects, because the relatives were distant. We have Honour, Robert's mother. But the time and expense . . .' Montgomery spoke in crisp, clinical tones, but inside the agitation was tightening its grip. Even if Honour could be protected from this new uncertainty, Theresa would have to be approached, if only to provide the names of Robert's doctor and dentist . . . 'No,' he continued, 'the dental avenue will be the simplest if McPherson was a regular attender.'

'Or we could approach this from the other side,' suggested William Bird. 'Check the corpse's teeth against Geoff Crabbe's records?'

'I don't like that idea. Monica would have to be involved, and it may prove to be a false alarm. Let's continue to concentrate on McPherson, but move on to Crabbe if we can't get hold of any X-rays or dental charts.' He sat down thoughtfully at the desk. 'Jackson said that Andrew Dunster claimed to have a hold over McPherson, something Crabbe could use as a lever. Let's say for the sake of argument that Crabbe was blackmailing McPherson, and was stepping up the pressure to do something McPherson didn't want to do. McPherson in desperation decides to kill Crabbe. He hits him over the head when Crabbe arrives at ten, but can't bring himself to continue the violence when he finds Crabbe is still alive. Every facet of his personality is against it . . .

'Crabbe is lying there unconscious. McPherson decides to inject him with lethal drugs then burn the place down very thoroughly to hide the evidence. News of a serial arsonist had been in the papers, and the death would be attributed to the fire. The coroner would bring in a verdict of accidental death, and Theresa would be able to collect both the insurance on the business and any existing life insurance on Robert while he was lying low. How am I doing, Will?'

'It sounds very plausible, sir. It would certainly explain the locked doors, and the fact that no needle was found in the body. But it's Theresa who bothers me. She seems genuinely devastated. Either she's a very good actress, or . . .'

'Or she's crying for Crabbe,' said Montgomery.

'I've seen Theresa,' said Ros Winger to Montgomery at two forty. 'She wasn't at the flower shop – she only works there part time. Mornings and all day every other Saturday. So I went to her home. She'd just arrived. I was surprised how untidy the house had become – it was immaculate before.

'I said to her we needed a few extra checks before the body could be released for burial, and she seemed to accept that. But when I asked about Robert's dental records, she told me he had always been afraid of the dentist, and hadn't attended for years.'

'Stalling,' murmured William Bird.

'After a lot of hesitation she gave me the name of his doctor, and a name she thought might have been his dentist, years ago. We went into the kitchen for a cup of coffee and I kept my eyes open as you suggested, sir. There didn't *seem* to be an inordinate amount of food anywhere for one person, but of course most of it was in the cupboards. I got a peek in the fridge when she opened it for milk, and there was very little inside – just some salad things, a bit of ham and cheese and a couple of yoghurts. She let drop in the conversation that she shops in the Spar round the corner, and is probably going there later this afternoon.'

'Were there any hints at all of male occupancy?' asked Montgomery.

'Not really. I asked if I could use the bathroom, but there was no shaving gear out on the ledge, and no smell of after-shave. There *were* two toothbrushes, but only one was damp. At the bottom of the bath there was a green wicker box for linen. I went through the clothes inside very quickly, and they were all female except for a pair of men's socks at the very bottom. That wouldn't be unreasonable: it's still less than a week since he died.'

Ros pushed back a strand of her blonde hair. 'I tiptoed to the bedroom to see about dents in the pillows, but the bed was already made and smoothed down. There were no scattered socks or items of male underwear, and no tea mugs on either of the bedside units. I didn't have long to look, though.'

'Thank you, Ros. Did you miss lunch? Sorry. I'll treat you next time we're both in the canteen.'

'How patronizing,' sniffed Jackson. 'You wouldn't do that for one of us.'

'Yes, I would. I distinctly remember buying you one of your favourite "strangler's delight" curries at the Lion and Lamb the other week.'

'That's different. That was out in the field.'

'I don't mind being patronized,' smiled Ros, 'but only as far as a cup of tea, thanks.'

'To calm your outraged sensitivities,' said Montgomery to the five detectives present, 'tea is on me for all of you. Now, ignoring Robert McPherson for the moment, why is Theresa still on her own in her hour of need? Why haven't her family come to support her?'

'There's only a sister,' said Ros, 'and she's in France, just about to have a baby. They were fostered as children after their parents split up, and Theresa has no local family she can appeal to. She's very shy; I don't think she has many friends.'

'Mm.' Montgomery couldn't make up his mind about Theresa. Perhaps she was simply a passive partner in all this. But whose partner? He had a theory to test . . . 'Any progress with your search for Crabbe's mistress?' he asked Jackson.

'No, sir. We're beginning to think it might be a false name.'

'Right. Here's what I want you to do. Take this photo out to Vera Blenkinsop in Bramton, and ask her if this is the man she saw with Theresa in the tea-shop. *Don't* involve Honour McPherson. If she's at Vera's place for any reason, you'll have to think of an excuse. You're checking the name of Robert's doctor, or something like that.

'You've got a different job, Graham. I want you to keep a discreet eye on Theresa McPherson's home for the rest of this afternoon. If she goes to the Spar, follow her and try to see what she's buying. Okay?'

'Yes, sir.'

'Anyone else want to mention anything?'

DC Grange raised a beefy paw. 'I've had some info from the plods who were doing house-to-house enquiries in Furlong End,' he said with a leer at Ros. 'First, that blue Fiesta was spotted by several people during the late evening and was probably there the whole time. At nine fifteen two separate people saw not only the Fiesta down the side passageway but a woman walking to the back of the shop.'

'Any description?'

'Very little. Thinnish, with a headscarf. But there's more.

One of these witnesses was on the opposite side of the road, and she says the driver of a Fiat was acting strangely nearby. This was a youngish blonde girl. She slowed the car, stopped it and peered across at the pharmacy for at least a minute. The witness doesn't know what happened next because she walked on past and turned up a side street to reach her own home. I'm assuming that the girl in the car was Judy Pearce, sir.'

'Yes,' agreed Montgomery. 'It's funny, though – she never mentioned any headscarfed woman to us.' He was troubled; this was consistent with Judy's apparent failure to spot the Fiesta. Glenn had seen it, and now they had statements to the same effect from independent witnesses. Judy had misled them – why?

'There's some other information,' went on Grange. 'The gang of boys hung around in that general area long after Glenn Foley left them at ten thirty. They don't have a collective name, but their leader is a seventeen-year-old called Jordan Hardwick who always wears a flamboyant red necktie. We interviewed him on Tuesday and he said he left the area at eleven, but it turns out they were seen as late as eleven thirty by a man who lives across the road. Hardwick himself and another boy also appear on the fire brigade video which was shot at twelve thirty, at the height of the blaze.'

'You saw this yourself?'

'Yes, sir. The film was better quality than last time. Hardwick was clear, the other boy less so.'

'Good.' The local fire brigade had recently introduced an experimental scheme whereby the onlookers at a major blaze were secretly videoed, and the films studied for recurring faces. Montgomery was hoping this pilot scheme would succeed, and become permanent. 'Find out as much as you can about Jordan and his gang before you approach him again,' he said.

As they headed for the canteen, Sergeant Bird drew level with Montgomery. 'It seems we were right about Judy,' he said. 'What do you want to do?'

'Have some more words with her,' Montgomery answered. 'Find out why she lied.'

Smythe peered round a tall pyramid of detergent boxes, a wire basket hung over his forearm. Theresa was shopping distractedly, doubling back and pausing for long periods before making her choices, and his role as a shadow was not being made easy.

So far he had noticed bread, cereal, a bag of apples and some broccoli in her basket. The quantities were inconclusive, and could equally well be for two people as for one. He was waiting for some key item like a pork chop, or a frozen dinner for one. In the meantime, his own basket swung empty.

Another customer, an ample woman with rosy cheeks, gave him an enquiring half-smile, and Smythe hurriedly seized a box of washing powder to avoid suspicion. He rounded the corner and edged his way past an elderly couple who were 'Sunday driving' in the aisle. Theresa was by the meat counter – now was his opportunity!

He pretended to compare various pieces of lamb's liver at one end of the pre-packed section while she stretched to pick up something further along. It was a flash-fry steak, quite a large one. He exchanged his liver for kidneys, frowned, and returned to his original piece of liver, waiting to see if she took a second steak.

She didn't; she moved on and began to delve in the frozen cabinet. Smythe seized his chance: he didn't want this washing powder at all; he would take it back!

Just as he was replacing the box, the rosy-cheeked woman gave him a beaming smile. 'I thought you didn't look very sure,' she said. 'It's so difficult, isn't it, deciding which one to buy? There's so much choice these days. Too much, if you ask me.'

But I didn't, thought Smythe, murmuring a platitude nevertheless.

'That's such a nice shirt you're wearing: would you call it

mulberry? You could ruin that with the wrong powder. You don't want anything that lists bleach or "brighteners" . . . See this little panel here: "ingredients". That's what you want to look for. Then you know what you're getting.'

'Thank you,' said Smythe, edging away.

She followed. 'I always use a liquid myself – this one. I say to myself it *must* be kinder, with nothing to dissolve. And it hasn't got any of those enzymes that can make you itch.'

'I'll try that,' said Smythe in desperation, and took a bottle. Theresa could be half-way out of the shop by now. Montgomery would have his pelt . . .

The woman still stood in his way. 'I could tell you wanted to know and were afraid to ask,' she said comfortably. 'There's no need to be embarrassed, though. I still have to ask things. Only the other day –'

'Thanks again,' gasped Smythe and turned tail. This aisle, like the other, ended near the single check-out; perhaps Theresa was still in the queue.

She was: three places ahead. Smythe craned shamelessly as she decanted purchases from the basket. The steak had no companion. The frozen fish fillets could be eaten individually. So did that prove Theresa was alone at home?

Ruefully he acknowledged that it didn't. The steak could be cut into two. Nothing else provided a genuine clue. Montgomery might well require him to repeat this wretched exercise . . .

Even more ruefully he studied the bottle of liquid detergent. His mother didn't use this brand, he knew. She loved enzymes and brighteners – and *she* did the family washing. He'd catch some trouble there, for sure!

'Judy's down at Westwood, playing tennis,' said Mrs Pearce when the two detectives appeared on her doorstep.

Westwood was Montgomery's own club, a place where he played elegant and intelligent squash against a variety of lumbering opponents. Having seen unstoppable paunches erupt on so many of his contemporaries, he was determined to stay fit.

Judy was embroiled in a fierce mixed doubles rally; they watched from the shadow of a sycamore as she leapt athletically from side to side, finally securing the point with a crisp backhand volley. Minutes later the game was finished; handshakes were exchanged across the net and the players wandered in separate pairs towards their kit.

Montgomery caught Judy's attention as she leaned over to unzip her bag and extract a towel. 'Can we talk for a few minutes?' he asked.

Alarm flickered in her eyes. 'Again?' she said after a pause.

'We need to clear up one or two areas of slight confusion,' he said.

'Just a minute...' She dried her glistening face with the towel, making a long business of it, and peeled the band from her wrist. 'Er... may I have a drink first?'

'Of course. We can talk back at your home if you prefer –'

'No!' she cut in with vehemence, then repeated more quietly, 'No. That wouldn't be a good idea. How about that table over there?' She pointed to a bench-style table close to the deserted outer tennis court. Minutes later they were all seated there, and Sergeant Bird was handing round the orange juice.

Montgomery spoke. 'It has become apparent that Robert's Fiesta was parked in the courtyard behind the shop all night, and was clearly visible up the side passageway. You told us you were actively wondering whether Robert was inside in order to warn him about the gang of boys... How come you failed to see his car?'

'I don't know. The light wasn't very good by then.'

'But there was a security light at that side of the building. We understand it was working perfectly well.'

'I'm sorry. I simply didn't see the car.'

'Could this have anything to do with the woman who entered the pharmacy?'

They saw the involuntary quiver of her pupils, the erratic pattern of her breathing. Helplessly she looked at each of the detectives in turn, but their faces were calm and unresponsive. She lowered her eyes and took a clumsy gulp of orange juice. 'What woman?' she said.

'Judy . . . two separate witnesses saw a woman walking up the side passage to the pharmacy at nine fifteen on Saturday. One of them saw you staring at this woman for a significant period of time from your car across the road – yet you never mentioned any of this to us. Why not?'

Judy knitted her fingers together. 'Inspector . . .' she said slowly. 'What if I was to say that I know this woman is irrelevant to your enquiry, and I was only trying to avoid trouble for her and misdirection for you . . . would you be prepared to leave it at that?'

'That's not a choice we can make in a possible murder enquiry, Judy. Everything is relevant until proved otherwise. A girl of your intelligence must be aware of that.'

She flushed behind the healthy outdoor glow. 'It's just that – I *know* this is nothing to do with Robert's death. She went away again after only a few minutes, and Robert was still alive.'

'You saw him?'

'I . . .' Judy wriggled in discomfort, suddenly aware that she was now compromising herself.

'Was the woman Theresa, Judy?' Montgomery's voice was very gentle.

She was silent, her head hung low.

'Shielding someone won't work in the long run.'

She blinked and bit her lip.

'Please help us.'

The 'clock' of tennis balls on the occupied courts sounded very distant. Even in the dappled sycamore shade the air was hot and thick. A hopeful bee hovered and landed on the rim of Judy's glass, but she gave no sign of noticing it.

At last she raised her eyes to Montgomery's face. 'It wasn't Theresa,' she said. 'I've never met her. No, the woman I saw was Margaret.'

12

'Would you like to give your mum a ring?' asked Sergeant Bird as he led the girl into the interview room.

'It's all right, thanks. She wasn't expecting me back for hours.' Judy, now showered and changed, glanced around the clean, bare interior with approval. Soon they were joined by Montgomery, and Judy was encouraged to elaborate on the story revealed at the squash club.

'I recognized Margaret quite easily,' she began. 'Her walk, the headscarf she wears . . . If I'd been on that side of the road I'd probably have called out to her from the car.'

'I had no idea why she was there, but I thought either she'd arranged to meet Robert late for some reason, or like me she'd spotted the dispensary light and wanted to check the property. She went up the side quite crisply and round to the back door. I was in two minds whether or not to follow. I didn't want to barge in on them, but my own evening had been a bit of a damp squib and I wasn't really ready to go home. After a bit of vacillation I parked the car further along the road, locked it and headed for the pharmacy myself.'

'Excuse me – did you see anything of the gang of boys at this point?'

'No. They'd gone.'

'Thank you. Do carry on.'

'The back door was unlocked. I slipped inside, into the store room.' She sent them an enquiring look. 'You know the layout? Downstairs there was the shop, the dispensary, a little washroom and a store-room extension. Upstairs was the rest room with a kettle, a sink and a fridge, plus another room for stock.

'I could hear voices, and they sounded strained. Margaret was doing most of the talking, and Robert was giving her short answers. I stepped into the shop, and was just about to cough to announce my presence when I began to hear their actual words.

' "You know it's right," she was saying in a queer, insistent way. "It's what should have always been. We both understand retail pharmacy. Together we can win through." Then he said something like, "Margaret, stop this, please. I have to work," and she said, "I understand, I'll help you," and he answered, "You understand nothing. Please go away. I'm busy." He sounded really agitated, but she didn't seem to notice. Eventually he told her that Theresa was coming in half an hour. For a few seconds no one spoke, then she gave a sort of short, bitter laugh. "You expect me to believe that? She never comes near the pharmacy these days. She's not interested in your problems."

'I must admit I thought it unlikely myself that Theresa would come to Furlong End at ten o'clock at night. She doesn't drive a car, and Robert had given the impression that she was nervous after dark. It sounded like an excuse to get rid of Margaret, and she saw through it. She started to *wheedle*; it was really embarrassing. Then she said . . .' Judy flushed and hesitated.

'Go on, Judy.'

'She said, "You're determined to pretend you don't understand. I'm not talking about a business partnership. Heaven knows, I don't have the funds. I'm talking about love! Robert, I've always loved you. Deep in your heart, you must know! Just as you know that your marriage is a sham. If I was your wife, you wouldn't have to pay me any wages. We'd sort everything out, share every problem, move forward together . . ." I felt terrible, standing there listening. I began to back away down the stock room, but I could still hear them. Suddenly a lot of things I'd dismissed as little quirks of Margaret's made sense. The way she'd always insisted on making his tea, or taking it to him if I'd made it . . . the way she'd seize any excuse to lean over a prescription with him, to be near him . . . There was never any hint of reciprocation. I don't think he even noticed.

101

'Anyway, I tried to get out of the building before I heard any more, but their voices were raised, even Robert's. He said something like, "I'm sorry, Margaret, I can't cope with this just now," but she ignored that and went on like a – bulldozer. I wondered if she'd been drinking. I'd almost reached the door when I heard Robert snap. He shrieked at her, "Get out! Get out, you ridiculous woman!" and I knew I didn't have time to fiddle with the door. I slipped behind a row of vertical shelves and ducked down.

'Margaret blundered through the store room, breathing heavily. I risked a glance from behind some boxes of cotton wool, and I saw her face . . . she was baring her teeth in a kind of snarl. I suppose it was the shock. When she'd gone, there was no sound from the dispensary. I waited two or three minutes for Margaret to leave the area, then let myself out as quietly as I could. I don't know if Robert heard the door; he didn't call, or anything . . . I went back to my car and drove away as quickly as possible.'

'*Was* there any sign of Theresa?' asked Montgomery.

'No.'

'What do you think, Will?' said Montgomery when Judy had signed a statement and left. 'A woman scorned after bottling all that up for eight years. Margaret must have nurtured hopes ever since the time Robert took her to Honour's house.'

'Yes. She would have felt dreadfully humiliated. But enough to return and murder him? I suppose it's not beyond the bounds of credibility.'

'She has keys to the place. Even if he locked the door after Judy had left, Margaret could have got back inside. And she knew about those stocks of anaesthetics. There's only one fly in the ointment – if this was a simple revenge killing, why did Geoff Crabbe disappear at exactly the same time?'

'He had an appointment at ten. Perhaps he saw something, and she had to deal with him as well.'

'One body, Will.'

102

'Mm. That does rather complicate matters. Does Margaret have a car?'

'I have no knowledge of one. She walks to work. We'd better check that. In fact, let's find out what we can about Margaret from other sources before we approach her directly. That neighbour of hers, perhaps – Glenn Foley's mother.'

That night, Montgomery found the familiar merry-go-round whirling in his brain. The case was becoming more complex, spreading like an infestation beyond the simple, clean lines of enquiry he liked to establish. It *would* be solved, he was confident. To allow himself to think otherwise could become a self-fulfilling prophecy of failure. But with limited manpower and so many avenues to explore, it could be weeks or even months before the truth was known – time during which the innocent parties, whoever they were, went on suffering.

'Why not read a bit more of your book?' suggested Carole, seeing his faraway look. 'How are you getting on with it?'

'Oh, I haven't been looking for deep meanings and symbols of "existentialist thought". I've just been reading it as a straight story.'

'No reason why not. It's well written, isn't it? Deceptively simple. Golding went on to win the Nobel Prize for Literature in the eighties . . . Would you like a cup of tea?'

'No, thanks.' Unlike Carole, Montgomery found that tea after about eight at night kept him awake later.

'Cocoa, then?'

'Now you're talking.' The living-room was quiet when she left. The children were upstairs, applying themselves to half-term homework, and the television had been turned off a few minutes earlier. He padded to his bedroom, fetched the book and returned to the sofa, only to see the bookmark slide to the floor.

Mentally he recapped the story as he turned the leaves in search of his place. The spectacles of Piggy the fat asthmatic boy had become a symbol of power, though never for Piggy himself. Even more important than the conch shell, which sanctioned its holder to address the other boys *en masse* without interruption, the glasses were a means of creating fire. Fire meant signals, warmth, cooked food . . . As tensions grew between the factions, Montgomery predicted that the spectacles would be fought over.

He found his place and began to read, but soon stopped again. Piggy without his thick spectacles was helpless, a prisoner of his poor eyesight. Supposing Robert McPherson had been similarly afflicted . . . The remains of the glasses found on the body had been identified as his; if he had put them on to Crabbe's face in order to mislead investigators, would he then have had sufficient visual acuity to lock the door and perform other, more complex tasks? It would have been vital for him not to arouse suspicions in any passer-by.

Perhaps there had been a spare pair, thought Montgomery. He must add this point to the list of enquiries. If such a pair were to be found, that would surely constitute another small indication that Robert McPherson was dead.

'I went to Bramton yesterday,' said Jackson the following morning. 'I showed Crabbe's picture to the Blenkinsop woman, and she gave a positive ID. She's confident that he was the man sharing coffee and canoodlings with Theresa McPherson three weeks ago.'

Montgomery was excited by this vindication. 'Did she say anything else?' he asked.

'She expressed disappointment that I wasn't William.' He turned to Sergeant Bird. 'She said she had a little surprise for you – something she'd forgotten to show you last time.'

'Did she specify?' enquired Sergeant Bird amid whoops and howls.

'She called it her *Streptococcus*, but I may have got that wrong. It was an indoor plant with blue flowers and hairy leaves.'

'*Streptocarpus*,' muttered William Bird. 'The Cape primrose.'

'Is there anything to report on the alibis of Sean Turner and Andrew Dunster?' asked Montgomery of the detectives as a whole. He couldn't dismiss the possibility that Crabbe and his associates had acted in concert.

'I checked the nightclub, Josie's,' growled DC Colin Haslam. 'They remember Sean Turner from Saturday night. He made some sort of ill-tempered scene around eleven, just after he arrived, and they nearly chucked him out. He stayed on though, and the bar staff can vouch for him between eleven and one.'

Eleven, thought Montgomery. That was the very earliest estimate for the start of the fire, and Furlong End was a good fifteen minutes' drive from the city centre. It looked as if Turner was in the clear by a small margin.

'I showed them Crabbe's mugshot,' went on Haslam, 'just in case he was one of their regulars, but they'd never seen him before. No one seems to know where he was on Saturday night. He left his golfing friends at seven o'clock.'

'How about Dunster?'

'I visited the sister,' said Jackson. 'She swore she was watching telly with Andrew all Saturday night while their parents were away for the weekend, but she looks as shifty as he does, and I'd take her story with a pinch of salt.'

'I suppose none of the witnesses who noted the Fiesta saw anybody answering the description of Crabbe, Turner or Dunster lurking near the pharmacy?' asked Montgomery. 'No, I didn't think so.'

In the background a telephone rang, and William Bird moved to answer it. They heard him give slow, deliberate replies, his mellow voice calm and soothing.

Smythe had just described his surveillance of Theresa McPherson when Sergeant Bird returned. 'That was Honour McPherson,' he informed them. 'She wanted to know if we'd made any progress.'

'It should be Theresa who's asking that,' observed Smythe. 'Why isn't she?'

'She may not want to give trouble,' allowed Montgomery.

'Honour is quite a different character; she doesn't baulk at issuing requests or commands . . .'

Grange was the next to report. 'Jordan Hardwick admits to watching the fire,' he said. 'However, he categorically denies starting it. He wouldn't divulge the identity of the boy seen with him on the video – said that on a "need to know" basis I had no need to know, because they were innocent. Cheeky young pup! He's actually quite bright. He's stayed on at school to do two A-levels. Christ knows why he heads a gang which pursues such deadbeat activities. Some kind of protest, perhaps? Anyway, he says he has no connection with the glue-sniffers whose hut was fired back in March. It's difficult to pin anything on him, sir.'

Montgomery nodded. 'Right; well, keep trying.' He issued various instructions to his team before turning towards his own office. 'One final point,' he said, pausing half-way. 'Will those of you tracking down Robert McPherson's medical and dental records please try to expedite matters?' As William Bird accompanied him to the door, he added *sotto voce*,' . . . Because it would be extraordinarily helpful to know who the corpse is.'

At Montgomery's behest, Sergeant Bird parked well down the road from Kathleen Foley's house. Margaret Kendall was probably at work, but they didn't want to alarm her, or risk her grilling Kathleen about the substance of their questions.

Glenn was at home with his mother, so Montgomery took the opportunity to include him in the conversation. 'We're still seeking background information on everyone connected with Mr McPherson,' he explained to them both. 'Little things one might normally dismiss can affect the actions and motivations of others . . . With that in mind, we felt we should establish the exact relationship between Robert and Margaret. Did she ever suggest that there was something special about it?'

'She did once,' said Kathleen. 'Years ago, when her father

was still alive. She'd just started working at the pharmacy – well, let's say she was a few months into the job – when she began dropping coy little hints about her and Robert becoming a couple, saying, "Watch this space," and things like that. The following year, though, I heard he'd married someone else, so I assumed that any romantic association with Margaret had fizzled out. If indeed it had ever existed.'

'Is she your closest friend in this area?' asked Montgomery.

'No,' said Kathleen hastily. Flushing a little, she added, 'Mike and Julie Bentall next door are our real friends. We go out a lot together.'

'Margaret's just an acquaintance, perhaps?'

'Well . . . we're friends in a way. I mean, I've known her a long time . . .' Kathleen Foley seemed to be struggling.

'She's weird,' said Glenn. 'Weird and pushy and interfering.'

'Glenn!'

'Well, it's true, isn't it? She always pokes her nose into whatever we're doing.'

'She's just interested, Glenn. She's always been very kind to you.'

'She interferes. She invites herself to things – Sunday lunch and Christmases and bonfires.'

'We've discussed this before. Margaret is lonely, and sharing what we have is the Christian thing to do.' Now Kathleen was scarlet with embarrassment.

'But she ruins all our fun. Especially Dad's. She always insists on lighting the bonfire herself, *and* half the fireworks! She spoils everything.'

Montgomery leaned forward. 'Is this true, Glenn – about the bonfire?'

'Yes,' answered the boy disgustedly. 'She gets all *excited* and intent, and no one else can have a go.'

13

'Margaret was ever so slightly sloshed,' said Emily Middleton with a reminiscent twinkle. 'We were drinking sherry while we priced all the goods for the bazaar. It was a long job, and we got through at least two glasses – probably three. I knew she didn't have to drive anywhere. In fact, she stayed on for dinner and my husband opened a bottle of wine. I suppose she must have left around nine.'

'Did she say if she was going straight home?' asked Montgomery.

'She implied that she was. Eric offered to escort her, but she declined. She was walking perfectly steadily, even though her emotions had loosened, as it were. No – I don't recall her mentioning any other destination . . .'

'Yes, I know Margaret Kendall,' said the proprietor of the off-licence, a heavy-set man with tobacco-stained teeth. 'She likes a chat, does Margaret. And a drop of sherry; Croft's her favourite. But not spirits – no, sirree.'

'Did she pop in last Saturday?'

'Saturday?'

'That was the night of the fire at the pharmacy.'

'I know. I was thinking . . . it's been longer than that, I reckon. Maybe a fortnight.'

'Are you sure of this? Were you on duty yourself?'

'I was here all right. Apart from half an hour when my nephew was covering. But that was around nine . . .'

'Does your nephew know Margaret Kendall by sight?'

'Well . . . I dunno, really. He *might*. But he's not in here as often as I am.'

While Montgomery curbed his exasperation, William Bird

saw a practical way forward. 'Your till roll will have recorded the purchases,' he said. 'May we see the records for Saturday night? We believe she may have bought a bottle of sherry here.'

After much fuss, grumbling and delay, the roll was produced. Coughing moistly from within the blue fug from his own cigarette, the man ran a pen past each price printed out between eight and ten o'clock. 'No sherry,' he pronounced at last. 'None of any brand.'

'May we take the roll?'

'As long as I get it back.'

In the front of their car, Montgomery and his sergeant studied a street map of the locality.

'The direct way back from Emily Middleton's house would take Margaret straight past the precinct,' observed William Bird. 'Returning via the off-licence, though, would have ensured that she missed the precinct by a matter of three or four hundred yards.'

'I expect she was hoping that no one would ask for her movements that night. But we did, so she had to spin the tale of the off-licence. Drinking sherry with Mrs Middleton probably put the idea into her head.' Montgomery leaned back and stretched his limbs. 'So what did happen, I wonder? Did she go to the pharmacy by prearrangement or did she, like Judy, spot the dispensary light and decide to investigate?

'And after her quarrel with Robert – what then? Did she storm off home and spend the rest of the night simmering with humiliation . . . ?

'Or did she return to extract her revenge?'

'It's for you,' said Smythe. The telephone was equidistant from his desk and Jackson's, but he was always the person expected to answer it. He pressed his slender fingers to the mouthpiece and hissed, 'Andrew Dunster.'

'Well, well.' Jackson's expression was one of self-satisfaction as he took the receiver. 'Andrew,' he said in encouraging tones. As Smythe watched, a cynical smile unfurled itself across his colleague's face. '. . . I'm pretty busy, but I suppose I could manage it,' said Jackson after a long pause. 'One o'clock, then. The Magnet?' That was the nearest pub to Geoff Crabbe's barn.

There was a kind of yelp from the other end.

'Keep your hair on,' went on Jackson. 'All right – the Three Bells.' He replaced the receiver. 'Dunster's running scared,' he said to Smythe. 'He thinks his repellent little hide is in danger, and he'll be arrested as an accessory. Wants to spill the beans without Turner listening in . . .

'This could be interesting.'

The Three Bells was a pleasant seventeenth-century country pub whose interior gleamed with horse brasses and copper warming pans. It was quiet, with just four men eating lunch and a handful of drinkers at the bar. At first, Jackson could see no sign of Andrew Dunster, but a complete circumnavigation of the ground floor eventually led him to a small table tucked away in an alcove behind a moth-eaten oak beam. Here sat his quarry, peering at a wrist-watch.

Jackson strode forward and Dunster started, his eyes rolling like those of a terrified horse. 'It's you,' he gasped.

'You did invite me.'

'Yes . . .' He waved an urgent hand towards the vacant seat. 'Sit down here. Quick. Are you sure Sean hasn't followed you?'

'I've been nowhere near Sean. I've come straight from the station.'

'Right . . . good.' He made a visible effort to control himself. 'I haven't got very long. He thinks I've gone to the bank . . . where are you off to?'

'The bar. I'm having a drink.' Jackson assessed the dregs of Dunster's glass. 'You want another of those?'

'For God's sake!'

'We'll look mighty suspicious if we're not drinking.'

'I suppose . . .'

Minutes later Andrew Dunster was leaning forward across the table. 'Before I start, you've got to tell me something. That man Montgomery – does he make deals?'

'All the time,' lied Jackson airily.

'He'll get me off if I tell you all I know?'

'He'll do his best for you.'

Dunster hesitated, his eyes flicking between the warped oak beam and the low wooden door of the lavatories opposite. 'It's Sean,' he said in a rush. 'He's got this – this Bowie knife. He said he'd slit me if I said anything to anyone. Then he pretended it was all a joke. It wasn't, though! I know it wasn't. Sean never jokes. He'd gone all pale and intense, like he does before he beats someone up . . .'

'What've you got for us, Andrew?'

He took a sip of whisky. 'Those drugs,' he said. 'Those Bulgarian imports . . . they were just the start. Geoff has some others coming that aren't merely unlicensed, they're counterfeit. Major categories, too: non-steroidal anti-inflammatories, H2 antagonists – those are for ulcers – and hormone replacement therapy. All areas where drug failure wouldn't be immediately apparent in clinical terms, especially if other medicines were being prescribed at the same time.

'Geoff wanted me for my knowledge of retail pharmacy, especially in helping him to find outlets for these things. Robert had given me a stack of old PJs . . .'

'What?'

'The *Pharmaceutical Journal*. It's the Society's weekly rag. People have to join the Royal Pharmaceutical Society when they qualify – it's mandatory, so membership is split between the hospital and retail sectors.

'The Society has a body called the Statutory Committee who sit in judgement on pharmacists accused of misdemeanours – anything from leaving unqualified staff alone in their shops to flogging dangerous drugs without prescription. The proceedings of the committee are given regular coverage in the journal, and the full name and address of every offender is published. Geoff got me to compile a list of every bent pharmacist from Leeds to Bristol. We wanted those who'd had their knuckles rapped, but who hadn't actually been struck off. In Geoff's opinion, they'd already shown a "flexible attitude", and many of them wouldn't be averse to earning a bit of extra money on the side. He was going to test them out with the unlicensed drugs, then move on to the fakes.'

Jackson nodded. 'Last time we met you said you had a hold over McPherson,' he said slowly. 'That was why Geoff was confident he'd play ball . . . Okay – so how come he sacked you?'

'Er . . . mutual agreement. I was ready to move on.'

Jackson could be as shrewd as Montgomery when he applied himself; now he saw the light. Whatever 'dirt' Andrew Duncan had on McPherson was probably of his own making, but in an area where McPherson was unable to disprove complicity. He sat back and took a leisurely swig of beer. Across the grainy wooden table Andrew's flabby face wore a mulish mask. Best to leave this topic for now . . .

'What about the Dikes?' he asked.

Andrew shrugged. 'Once McPherson was in Geoff's pocket, he'd have had to supply those, of course.'

'Mm. How much of all this does Sean know?'

'Everything. He planned it with Geoff.'

'Did he know about the ten o'clock appointment?'

'Yes.'

'Did he say if he'd be going to Furlong End himself?'

'Not to me.'

'How often does he lose his cool?'

'Too often. He's got a vicious temper behind that sickly-looking exterior. He's surprisingly strong; I've seen him take on three. Yet he hasn't got any form for assault or ABH – he melts into the shadows as soon as the fuzz arrive . . .' Mention of Sean seemed to have alarmed Andrew. Nervously he shrank back in his seat and glanced at his watch. 'I've got to

112

go very soon. Tell me again about Montgomery. Can he be trusted? Will he keep me out of this?'

'He's even more trustworthy than I am,' replied Jackson.

'I've only just started working with Geoff,' rushed on Andrew. 'I've got nothing to do with any murder – I just want out of the whole situation. You can fix it, can't you?'

'I'll certainly try.'

'Listen . . .' Now his shallow blue eyes sharpened with a look of cunning more reminiscent of Sean. 'Tell Montgomery I've got something he wants. I'll deal if he will.'

'And what might that be?'

'Some information Sean said he was after.'

'Would you like to specify?'

'To Montgomery.'

Jackson sighed. 'Andrew, to all intents and purposes I'm Montgomery's agent, and I haven't much time either. I suggest you either put up, or shut up and take your chances.'

The blustering façade imploded and Dunster was once more a young man out of his depth. He chewed his knuckles, then dug a slip of paper from his pocket. With a final anxious survey of the immediate area, he slid it across the table to Jackson. 'Here,' he said. 'It's a copy of a diary entry of Geoff's. We keep a big diary in the office for general planning, as well as a wall chart. One day in March Geoff was chatting on the phone – quite coarse stuff, really. It was obviously to a woman: he harked back at one point to the way they'd been dancing at some New Year's Eve party. He had his feet up and he was doodling with a pen as he spoke. I saw him decorating a word in one of the margins, and later I took a proper look. It said "Shona", and there was a row of digits underneath.'

Jackson glanced down at the paper. 'These,' he said.

'Yes. I think it's a telephone number.'

'So?'

'*So?*' repeated Dunster angrily. 'So Montgomery wants the mistress.'

'I see. We were given the name Barbara Leadbetter.'

'By Sean?'

'Yes.'

'He was probably having you on.'

Little termite, thought Jackson. Aloud, he said, 'Does Geoff have more than one ladyfriend?'

'I think that's possible. He comes on strong to all the girls – it seems to be second nature to him.'

Jackson quaffed some more of his beer. 'Is there one called Theresa?' he asked casually.

'I don't know. There might be. Look, I must go. It's almost – hell!' His mouth gaped and his face contracted with fear. The next moment his underexercised body was squeezing a clumsy retreat into the cramped space beneath the table. The supporting column wobbled; the remnants of Jackson's beer slopped and surged in the glass.

Looking round unhurriedly, Jackson spotted a lean youth with black hair, deep-set eyes and a sour expression approaching their alcove. It was not Sean Turner. With a wry smile he rose, finished his drink and left the pub.

It was late that Friday when the detectives were once more clustered in the CID room. Neither funding nor manpower was available for much weekend work, but Montgomery was determined that the case should not hang in limbo. For all he knew, both a murderer and an arsonist were wandering round Nottingham, and at least one of these might strike again.

Jackson was the first to report, followed by Smythe. 'Theresa is still acting normally,' Smythe told them. 'She was at The Flower Bower this morning, then she called at the bank and the post office on the way home. She spent the afternoon inside . . .'

Montgomery wished he had the resources to keep a similar watch on Monica Crabbe. With mild irritation he enquired again about progress with the corpse's identity.

'There's a chink of light on that front,' said Grange. 'We couldn't track down McPherson's old dentist, but his GP has looked back in the notes and found that he suffered with sinusitis about fifteen years ago and had an X-ray taken at the Victoria. The hospital are trying to trace the film right now.'

'Good. That's something, anyway.'

After further discussion they filed out wearily, until only William Bird was left with Montgomery.

'How do you feel about some unpaid overtime, Will?'

'It staves off the boredom.'

Montgomery smiled. They both knew that William Bird, with his garden, his wall-to-wall collection of books and his classical music, was never bored. 'Tomorrow,' he said, 'I think we should visit some ladies.'

14

'Carole isn't best pleased,' confided Montgomery to William Bird as they drove towards Fielding Avenue the next day. 'We were supposed to do our Sainsbury shopping blitz together this morning. Still, she knows what murder investigations are like.'

'Didn't you say you were going out for dinner tonight?'

'That's right. Some friends in West Bridgford. I must make sure I'm back in time, with enough residual energy to be alert and entertaining. Carole hates it when I "switch off" in company.'

'Plenty of people never get as far as switching on,' observed William Bird drily. 'Left just here, sir . . .'

Montgomery parked the Sierra outside Margaret Kendall's faded-looking semi-detached. 'We were wondering if she had a car,' he recalled. 'At least there's a garage, but she may only use it for storage.'

The front door opened just as they approached; Margaret Kendall stood there with a bunch of small keys in her hand. 'Oh,' she said. 'Hello. I was just about to go shopping.'

'Locally?'

'No. Tesco.' That was two miles away. 'I can go later, though. Come inside.' Briskly she motioned them to seats. 'It's about Robert and the pharmacy, isn't it; have you some news?'

'We've made progress,' replied Montgomery, 'but one or two possible red herrings have sprung up, which we need to eliminate. I'm afraid one of them concerns you.'

'Me?' She looked aghast – and guilty.

'You were seen by three independent witnesses entering Furlong End Pharmacy at nine fifteen last Saturday night, yet you never mentioned this to us.'

He waited; she flushed a fiery red.

'I . . .' Her voice petered out in a croak.

'We understand there was an argument between yourself and Robert, and you left the pharmacy just before nine thirty.'

The silence was blistering; Margaret Kendall seemed to gasp for air. Eventually, with a great gulp, she spoke again. 'I don't know where you've got your information from. This is all such a shock.'

'Do you deny that you were there?'

'Yes . . . no . . . I . . . no. No, I don't.' Now the colour receded in a sluggish trickle, leaving her face grey and haggard. 'I did go to the pharmacy, but nothing happened there that will in any way aid your investigation.'

'We've been anxious to trace any sightings of Robert on that Saturday night,' said Montgomery with forbearance. 'Your evidence could be most important. Why did you suppress it?'

'The matter was personal, and embarrassing. I didn't want to give people the ammunition to laugh behind my back. It wasn't necessary . . . they didn't need to know.'

'Miss Kendall, you must tell us. Not to do so raises grave suspicions about your having a role in his death yourself.'

'Never!'

'Then clear yourself. We know you were with Emily Middleton until nine, and you'd drunk a bit of sherry. You elected to go home alone on foot, a route which would take

116

you straight past the pharmacy unless you had some reason for a diversion . . .?' He raised an eyebrow, and her gaze fell in shame.

'I didn't go to the off-licence,' she admitted. 'I only said that to avoid – this! I went home the normal way and saw that the dispensary light was on. I was feeling quite mellow and sociable, and I wondered if poor Robert was stuck in there on his own working late. I had my keys, but I knocked on the back door and once he knew it was me, he opened it. He seemed agitated and preoccupied, and I guessed he was worrying about money again. Suddenly I knew that this was the right time to propose that we enter a partnership which could solve all his problems. I'd had the idea for years.'

'Why should it be embarrassing for people to know that?'

'Well – he turned me down flat. So I left.'

Montgomery slowly nodded, as if understanding and waiting for more.

'That's it, Inspector. That's all I can tell you.'

'I see. You suggested a business partnership?'

'Yes.'

'Well, *I* suggest you are not telling the truth. You had a longstanding affection for Robert which you chose to declare last Saturday night with all the spurious confidence that sherry can induce. You wanted him to ditch Theresa and marry you. *That's* the proposal he turned down flat.'

She stared at him as if he were a warlock.

'How do you *know*?' she hissed.

'It's true, isn't it!'

Her lower lip quivered and jerked; helplessly she groped for a handkerchief, then burst into noisy sobs.

Sergeant Bird was used to parting with his clean linen handkerchiefs. He handed her a neatly ironed square, then waited.

'It's not right,' she slavered at last. 'All these years I've had to watch him . . . no support from *her* . . . it should have been me. I could have done so much for him – and now he's dead, and it'll never happen.'

'How did you feel when you left the shop?'

117

'Crushed . . .' She snorted into the handkerchief. 'Demeaned . . . he didn't want to hear what I had to say. He couldn't wait to be rid of me.'

'Margaret . . . did you go back again afterwards?'

Puzzled lines creased her brow. 'No. Of course not.'

'What did you do?'

'I went home.'

'Are you *sure* you didn't return for further words – or any other reason?'

Now she looked him in the face. 'Absolutely sure. What are you suggesting – that *I* burned the pharmacy down? My own place of work? I did not, and you can never prove such a thing!'

'All right, Miss Kendall. Tell us if you met anyone on your way home. Did you see a neighbour, or speak to anyone on the telephone?'

She paused. 'I'm sorry, I simply don't remember. My mind was on other things. I may have passed someone . . . I don't know.'

'And inside your house – were you alone?'

'Yes.'

'What did you do?'

'Found my own sherry bottle.'

A little later, Montgomery guided his catechism back to the subject of Robert's demeanour in the shop. 'You said Robert seemed agitated and preoccupied even as you arrived,' he stated. 'Can you amplify that at all?'

Margaret Kendall concentrated. 'I felt he was making preparations of some kind,' she answered.

'To do with papers?'

'I don't know. I just sensed that he was in the middle of something which wasn't merely accounts. But I didn't care. You're right about the alcohol. I just went ahead and said my piece regardless.' She was calmer now, but mortified.

'Did you see anything unusual in the dispensary?'

118

'Such as?'

'Anything like – a weapon, for instance.'

Her eyes widened. 'No. Nothing of that kind.'

'And did Robert indicate that he was expecting any other visitors that night?'

'He said Theresa was coming at ten, but I didn't believe him. She doesn't have a car. It was obvious he was trying to get rid of me.'

'Did he mention anyone called Geoff Crabbe?'

'Geoff Crabbe? No.'

The detectives prepared to leave. As Margaret Kendall escorted them through the hall, Montgomery turned to her. 'Robert's glasses,' he said. 'Did he keep a spare pair on the premises?'

'Yes,' she replied. 'In the desk drawer. He was as blind as a bat without them.'

Theresa McPherson, too, regarded Saturday as a natural time to go shopping. William Bird spotted her emerging from the Spar with two large carrier bags as they drove past to park near her home.

'May we help you?' he offered as she entered her front garden, and less than a minute later he was standing with Montgomery in her small square kitchen.

'I'll just put away the fresh and frozen foods,' said Theresa, 'then I can listen to what you've come to tell me. Would you like a cup of coffee?'

William Bird was feeling the familiar stomach rumblings he experienced when deprived of food for more than two hours at a stretch. Perhaps there would be biscuits . . . He glanced hopefully at Montgomery, but saw only a narrowing of the eyes and a subtle shake of the head.

'Thank you, but not just at present,' he said. As Theresa unpacked her carriers he saw, like Smythe before him, that none of her purchases pointed unequivocally to the presence of an extra person in the house.

119

'Now . . .' she said warily in her light voice as they sat in the living-room.

Montgomery was sombre. 'Our investigations into the death of your husband persistently indicate some involvement by a businessman called Geoff Crabbe. What can you tell us about this man?'

Theresa appeared confused. 'You asked me that before. I – I don't think I know the name.'

'Let me refresh your memory. This is the man who paid familiar attentions to you in a city centre tea-shop three and a half weeks ago. Geoff Crabbe, forty, only a year or so older than Robert . . . Is he your lover, Theresa?'

She clapped a hand over her mouth and began to tremble.

'We know he had an appointment at the pharmacy the night of the fire. We know he was trying to embroil Robert in criminal activity. We'd like to know his whereabouts now. Can you help us?'

She looked at him piteously, her shoulders sagging in defeat. 'I was hoping it wasn't true,' she said. 'I was praying it wasn't.'

'Is he your lover?' repeated Montgomery.

'No . . . but I was fond of him.'

'How did you meet him?' asked Sergeant Bird.

Her gaze slid to the floor. 'He came into The Flower Bower a few weeks ago when Mrs Zolbert was out at the back with a delivery van. He was pleasant and friendly; he made me laugh. The next time, he flirted a bit, even though I told him I was married. He didn't wear a wedding ring himself. Mrs Zolbert kept striding in and out with enormous frondy plants; she gave us evil looks and he nicknamed her Hecate. I didn't see any harm in chatting with Geoff . . . Everything in my life was so *serious*, so subdued . . . It was wonderful to find that someone with a sense of humour actually wanted to spend time with me.

'We had a little joke about him whisking me off and marrying me himself. It was going to be the Seychelles, or somewhere beautiful and remote like that . . . Eventually I did

120

agree to meet him in town, in a tea-shop. It felt – rather naughty and exciting. I wouldn't have hurt Robert for anything, but this was just a game. Geoff was still flirtatious, but we didn't do anything *wrong* . . . He asked me about my home life, and Robert, and his job. He asked if Robert ever cheated on his tax return, and I said, certainly not!

'We met once more in the same tea-shop, just a few days before Robert and I visited Newstead Abbey together. I remember mentioning our plans to Geoff, who said he'd be thinking of me, and how lucky Robert was . . .'

Her face, smoothly intent, began to craze into an expression of pain and bewilderment. 'I didn't expect to see Geoff at Newstead,' she went on. 'But suddenly he was there, watching us from the hedge near the Eagle Pond. Robert asked if I knew who it was, and I demurred. I felt he'd be sure to misconstrue the situation if I tried to explain. But I was terrified that Geoff would come and speak to me, and let on that we'd been in the tea-shop . . .'

Once more, Theresa was visibly trembling. 'Geoff did come towards us. He addressed Robert, then spoke to me as if we'd never met. I was both relieved and alarmed: I'm not very good at acting. Robert then took charge, instructed me to stay where I was and walked round the pool with Geoff.' She pressed her knuckles to her teeth. 'There was hostility between them – I could see it in their stance, in Robert's manner . . . I wondered if it was because of me, but when Robert came back, alone, he told me not to worry; Geoff had made him an unwelcome business proposition, he said, but the matter was now closed. He tried to act naturally; I could tell he was brooding, though, and the day was spoiled . . .'

She lifted her gaze to Montgomery, her eyes welling with moisture. 'I never saw Geoff after that. He didn't come to the shop again, and I didn't know where he lived. Inspector . . . do you really think Geoff had a hand in Robert's death? Do you?'

'It's certainly a possibility.'

She wiped away a tear. 'Robert was always so good to me,' she said. 'With him everything was quiet, and safe. But he hated to be touched, and he didn't like to touch other people, either. I thought I could change all that once we were married, but – he wouldn't let me. He'd shy away if I tried to cuddle him. My own husband! I think people were beginning to wonder why we had no children. Everyone except Honour . . . I'm sure she knew. It was the way she'd always treated him, and he'd learned the lesson well.

'Robert needed good order. Everything had to be in its place. I always found that difficult: I'm a naturally untidy person. When I arrange flowers, I make the most terrific mess. But the end result is what counts.

'Geoff released something in me – a sense of fun, of lightness and sunshine. Just for a few weeks I felt I had something to look forward to. Now I can see it was stolen sunshine . . .

'If Geoff killed Robert, Inspector, then so did I.'

'Let me find you a watering hole,' said Montgomery to his sergeant when they had left the house. 'I'm sorry I scotched your coffee; I don't like accepting hospitality from suspects.'

'Do you still consider Theresa a suspect? She seemed sincere to me.'

'So did Margaret Kendall; neither of them has an alibi. In some ways, this story of Robert as a cold, unsatisfactory husband makes it *more* likely that she'd want to be rid of him and throw in her lot with a character like Crabbe . . . Yet the ingenuous way she told us every detail – that would suggest innocence. Or an attempt to distance herself from Crabbe, despite what she said at the end.'

'Margaret Kendall put up an Aunt Sally.'

'Yes, she did. Suggesting she wouldn't have torched the pharmacy because it was her place of work. We know all about Green Triangle's head-hunting efforts. No, as things stand we have no proof at all that Margaret Kendall didn't return to Furlong End in a vengeful rage last Saturday . . .' Montgomery reached for his mobile phone and consulted a piece of paper. 'I'm just trying that number Andrew Dunster gave Brian.' He punched out the digits, and waited. 'No answer,' he said after a minute.

Sergeant Bird patted his stomach meaningfully. Montgomery smiled, nodded and started up the car.

'I've had a lovely evening,' said Carole, leaning back against the headrest as Montgomery drove the Sierra north across Trent Bridge. Below twinkled the lights of the Victoria Embankment, while through the open window wafted warm night air. 'You were in really good form – Diana and Clive were fascinated by your stories. In fact, Diana spent half the dinner ogling you across the candles. I think she fancies you.'

'Good taste, that woman,' said Montgomery. He was glad he'd made the effort; Carole deserved more than just a zombie at her side. She looked marvellous herself tonight in an emerald strapless dress, her thirty-eight-year-old body still lean and fit.

Calmly he negotiated the city traffic, his mind intermittently touching on the genial few hours shared with his wife and friends. The car purred east towards Carlton and home; would Justin be watching the late film when they arrived . . .?

Suddenly, Carole nudged his arm. 'Look!' she said. 'Over there . . . the sky.'

Montgomery looked. Above the familiar glow of neon streetlamps shimmered a new halo of burnished orange. Fire, somewhere in the suburbs . . .

'Sorry, Carole, but I must check this.'

'It's all right.' She hung on to the top of the seat belt as he swung off the main road and sped towards the sinister reflection. At the edge of an area of semi-detached properties, an isolated structure writhed like a living thing. Flames speared through the roof of a long flat wooden building, clawing their way up to the glaring canopy above, spitting and roaring as the attendant firemen desperately unwound the thick hose.

Montgomery pulled on the handbrake. 'Stay here,' he said

to Carole, then sprinted towards a helmeted fire officer he recognized.

'That was quick,' said Charnley.

'I was just passing. What is this place?'

'A garage, but it was abandoned. The owner's business went into liquidation months ago, although we understand a lot of inflammable stock was still on the premises. A local resident raised the alarm.' He squinted towards the gathering inferno, pinpoint images of flames dancing in his eyes. 'I reckon our pyro's been at it again – don't you?'

15

'Did we pull the cheetah's tail, I wonder?' said Sergeant Bird on the Monday morning.

'Stir someone into action, you mean? Yes – the thought had crossed my mind.' Montgomery looked down at the preliminary report compiled on the fire. Abandoned building, no casualties, evidence of arson, probable agent paraffin . . . He had seen the few onlookers for himself, but they had all been strangers. 'I didn't spot either of our ladies at the site, though,' he added.

'Whoever did it must have scarpered promptly. We've set up the usual enquiries.'

Montgomery's morning passed in an uphill trudge of paperwork, telephone calls and meetings, including the briefing of his superintendent. As he traversed the corridor back to the CID room, he felt drained and frustrated; however positively he presented his investigation to others, deep down he felt the crawling helplessness of time passing, of firm lines of enquiry becoming wavy and blurred. If only they could identify the body . . . everything else was waiting to follow.

'Any messages?' he asked the junior officers.

'We've been inundated,' replied Jackson. 'First Honour McPherson with her Royal Enquiry, then Monica Crabbe. She's really worried about Geoff. There's still been no word from him. She rang Sean at Morgifts on Saturday, and apparently he was most abrupt with her. He said something like, "I don't know anything and I don't want to know anything." After that Will's friend Vera Blenkinsop rang in.'

Sergeant Bird levered himself out of his chair. 'It was nothing much, sir, though Vera was excited. She primed a few of her cronies to ask around the village and see if anyone knew where Robert had gone when he left Honour's house that Saturday afternoon. She called them ladies "chosen for their discretion" . . . let's hope that's the case. Anyway, one of them told her yesterday that a friend saw him in Southwell Minster during Evensong.'

'Evensong? That's mid-afternoon, isn't it? About three o'clock.'

'Only on Sundays. Three fifteen. But weekdays and Saturdays in term-time it's at five forty-five. Apparently he was sitting on his own at the back with his chin on his chest, and he stayed there when everyone else filed out.'

'Is this lady sure it was him?'

'So Vera says. She thought you would be pleased – called it "the missing link".' He smirked. 'I must confess it made me think of apes and hominids.'

'Well, we did ask her for the information, although I'm not sure quite where it gets us. Perhaps he was planning how to handle Crabbe, and needed somewhere to think. Did you thank Vera?'

'Fulsomely. She said if we needed anything else, she was only too happy . . .'

Montgomery lifted a hand. 'I get the picture. Now . . .' Dimly he heard his own office telephone ring behind the glass panels. 'Excuse me.' He strode to answer it.

'Inspector Montgomery?'

'Speaking.'

'It's Margaret Kendall here . . .'

125

Margaret Kendall dealt with the morning flurry of customers as pleasantly and efficiently as she could. She had never believed in letting personal hurt stand in the way of duty, and the Green Triangle staff had been very kind. Nevertheless, she felt her smile freeze when she saw the shining blonde hair of Judy Pearce at the end of the queue.

When her turn came, Judy limped to the counter with a rueful grin. 'Hello, Margaret,' she said. 'I've been an idiot – pulled a calf muscle at Westwood. Have you got some Tubigrip, please?'

'You've time to play tennis, then,' said Margaret coolly as she rummaged in a drawer full of bandages.

'Well, yes. I haven't managed to sort out another job yet. I don't suppose they need any more help here?'

'Not that I'm aware of. No doubt they would advertise in the usual way.'

Now Judy seemed to notice the restrained welcome; her blue eyes flicked a quizzical glance at Margaret's face.

'Will this size be suitable?' went on Margaret, brusquely opening the packet to show the circumference of the support bandage.

'Fine, thank you.'

Wordlessly Margaret closed the box and wrapped it in a Green Triangle paper bag. She intoned a price, took Judy's money and handed her the change. The stampede of customers had quietened. Judy held her ground at the counter. 'Margaret, is something wrong?' she asked. 'Have I offended you?'

'You should know the answer to that.'

'I'm sorry, I don't.'

'You think by coming here you can pretend you haven't been telling Inspector Montgomery all kinds of lies about me?' She lowered her voice, but the sharp sibilance persisted. 'How else could he have made the wild guesses he did? Who else could have told him?'

126

'They weren't lies,' said Judy miserably. 'I did try to defend you.'

'*Defend* me? A young miss like you? How flattering!' She clenched her fists. '*What* a picture you must have painted, to give him the idea I had designs on Robert! How you must have extrapolated from the little things you saw – not to mention whatever you thought you saw. What was it? The fact that I liked to make his tea? The cosy chats about prescription charges and the Pricing Bureau? Well, let me tell you your prurient little interpretations were utter nonsense! Robert was a friend, that was all. I happen to have known him for nine years, as against your seven weeks. So I'd be obliged if you'd refrain from bending anyone else's ear with your malice on this subject – you understand?'

She felt more goaded than ever as an expression akin to relief passed over Judy's clear-cut features, but the girl answered neutrally enough. 'Of course, Margaret. I dare say the Inspector made a few assumptions of his own.'

As Judy limped towards the door, Glenn Foley opened it and stood aside to let her pass. Then he made his own way to the counter with a similar halting gait, his eyes fixed on a handful of coins he was counting. What *is* this? thought Margaret in irritation. A convention of the lame? Aloud, she said, 'Can I help you, Glenn?' He looked up in alarm, and hesitated. It was clear he had not expected her to be working there. 'Shouldn't you be at school?' she asked.

'Oh, er, yes, but the teacher has let me out to buy something. One of the boys in our chemistry class had an accident with the bunsen burner and he's hurt his arm. They haven't got the right sort of dressings in the sick room, so we wondered if you had any . . .'

'Has he been seen by a doctor?'

'It's not quite that bad. It just needs something to cover it.'

'Glenn, this sounds fishy to me. There's a pharmacy much closer to your school than this one. And why isn't a teacher or the secretary buying the dressing?'

She could almost see the cogs whirring as he struggled to

reply. 'Actually,' he whispered, 'it's my friend Roger. He did it at home yesterday with his chemistry set, and he doesn't want his mum to know because he was playing with it in the kitchen while they were out and he's not supposed to. He was heating copper sulphate – you know, the blue stuff, to drive off the water molecules and turn it into the white stuff, and then the oxide, which is black. It spat out at him and burned his arm. I said I'd try and get him something today. I thought if I went shopping too near the school someone would see me. You won't tell, will you, Miss Kendall? Please.'

Margaret was not convinced by the story. 'Your friend should get his arm seen to. He might have done permanent damage.'

'No, it's only the surface of the skin. I've seen it. All it needs is a dressing that won't stick, or leave fluffs . . .'

'How big is the burn?'

'About two inches long.'

'Right. Here's some melolin. One side is white, the other side is clear and looks like cellophane. You put the *clear* side against the skin. Do you want some tape, or a bandage to secure it?'

Glenn looked doubtfully at his money.

'I'll pay for it if you haven't got enough.'

'Oh – thanks. Just a loan, Miss Kendall – I'll pay you back.' He took all three items and walked towards the door, his gait still lopsided.

'What happened to your leg?' she asked.

'I twisted my ankle,' he mumbled. 'It's okay.' He left the shop; Margaret stared long and thoughtfully at his retreating figure.

Sergeant Bird parked the car just as Roger Pearce was arriving home from school. Alongside Montgomery he watched as the boy swung his briefcase with cheery abandon, chaffed with his friends by the gatepost and whistled his way up the path.

'Not much wrong with him,' observed William Bird.

128

'Glenn could have been talking about another Roger. It doesn't really matter. Roger Pearce can tell us what we want to know.'

'Do you think Margaret Kendall's suspicions will prove to be justified?'

Montgomery unclipped his seat belt. 'I've no idea, Will, but I'll tell you one thing – when she rang this morning, I rather hoped Miss Kendall was ringing to confess!'

It was Judy who opened the door. She looked suntanned and healthy, apart from a slight limp as she led them to the sitting-room. 'I saw you playing at Westwood yesterday evening,' she enthused to Montgomery. 'You were really good! You had that man running everywhere!'

'Trying to deny middle age, my wife would say,' he replied benignly. 'She's afraid I'll end up with either a pulled muscle or a heart attack on court.'

'Well, I'm nineteen and I've just pulled a muscle. I didn't warm up properly. I'd kick myself – if I could!'

They laughed, and Montgomery asked if Roger could spare a few minutes.

'Roger? I thought it was me you'd come to see.' Her face grew grave. 'He's not in any trouble, is he? Not Roger. He steers clear of all the rough elements in the class . . .'

'No, we only want some information from him.'

'He's upstairs changing. He just came in from school. Hang on, and I'll fetch him.'

'Thank you. By the way, does he have a chemistry set?'

Judy's astonished expression answered the question and soon her younger brother, wearing shorts, a clean yellow sweatshirt and a well-scrubbed face, appeared at the door to speak for himself. 'Please stay, if you don't mind,' Montgomery said to Judy, then proceeded to recount to Roger a potted version of the story Glenn had fed to Margaret. 'Does Glenn have any other friends called Roger?' he asked.

'No. I'm the only one in the school, apart from a boy in the first form.'

'Was Glenn referring to you, then, when he explained about the copper sulphate?'

By way of reply, Roger rotated his bare forearms for them to examine every inch of the skin. Not one blemish marred the caramel-tanned smoothness. He pulled the floppy sleeves up to his shoulders; his upper arms were similarly clear.

Montgomery sat unsurprised. He had already noted the absence of lesions on Roger's legs. 'What about Glenn himself?' he asked. 'Has he had any injuries recently?'

'He said this morning that he'd twisted his ankle, so he couldn't do athletics with us. For a while he stood by the track, then he disappeared and I didn't see him again until this afternoon.'

'Did he show you the ankle injury?'

'No, but he did seem cautious about putting his right leg down.'

'Roger, can you tell us Glenn's exact relationship with Jordan Hardwick?'

The boy shrugged and looked uncomfortable.

'It won't be sneaking, just getting some facts straight. We know quite a lot already about Jordan and his gang.'

'Go on,' whispered Judy.

'Well . . .' Roger hesitated, then took a big breath. 'Jordan's got a big reputation in school,' he said. 'The masters think he's an ace A-level student, but among the boys all these stories go round about things he's supposed to have done – anything from cat burglary to nicking a police motorbike. I'm not sure how many, if any, are true, but it gives him a certain . . .'

Cachet, thought William Bird.

'. . . You know, among the younger boys. Out of school he leads a gang of mainly fifth-formers. They don't have a collective name as such, but everyone knows them as "Jordan's set". They hang around at the bowling alley, the ice rink and the arcade when they've got money, or near the Furlong End precinct when they haven't. They seem pretty aimless to me, but Glenn is obsessed with them. He's been longing to join the gang, and asked me to go along with him. I told him I wasn't interested, and they wouldn't want younger kids like us tagging along in any case . . .'

Again he paused. Judy gave him an encouraging little nod.

'It turned out I was wrong. Glenn told me a few weeks ago that they would let him join if he passed some "initiation tests". I found it difficult to believe. Perhaps he'd pestered them to such a degree that they'd given in – or perhaps they were just playing with him. I've heard that Jordan can be sadistic. Either way, I didn't want to know. I tried to talk Glenn out of it, but he was so set on the idea I was wasting my time. So now we don't see much of each other.'

'Was he your friend before?'

'Well . . .' Roger screwed up his face and shifted uneasily in his seat. 'We used to be. It was mainly last year – we did some studying together in the library after school 'cause he was better at Latin than I was. In return I tried to teach him to play tennis, but he was hopeless – a complete rabbit. Then his mother said, why not study at their home? I went a few times, and she'd give me tea and chocolate cup-cakes, but soon she was pumping me about the youth club at St Felix's, and I realized she had a hidden agenda . . .'

No such thing as a free cup-cake, mused Sergeant Bird.

'I got the feeling she wanted me to take Glenn somewhere wholesome on Saturday nights, so he wouldn't fall in with bad company. She smothered him all the rest of the time, so I think she sensed he'd break out himself if she didn't provide him with a channel . . . I did take him along, but he was a bit of a pain and wouldn't join in anything. Eventually he stopped coming.'

'I see,' said Montgomery. 'Were you at the youth club last Saturday?'

'Yes. I was in a snooker tournament.'

'When did that finish?'

'Eleven.'

'He got home at twenty-past,' said Judy. 'Dad was

131

beginning to agitate, but he calmed down when Roger told him he'd come second in the play-offs.'

'Did you see Glenn at all, Roger, either at the club, or on your way home?'

'No. I'm sorry.'

Montgomery pondered for a moment. 'Did Glenn ever tell you if he'd embarked on the "initiation tests" to join Jordan's set?'

'He hinted that he had.'

'And did he ever describe to you the nature of these "tests"?'

For the first time, Roger's sincere face clouded. 'No, sir,' he answered. 'All I could gather was that they were dangerous, and they involved breaking the law.'

It was after hours when the detectives returned to the station, but William Bird followed as Montgomery let himself into a small deserted office and began to sort through a shelf full of video cassettes.

'That fire brigade video from Furlong End,' muttered Montgomery. 'Where is it?'

'Try the drawer underneath the monitor,' said William Bird.

Soon they sat hunched towards the flickering images which crossed the screen in blurred shades of grey. 'That's the best quality they can manage,' said the sergeant. 'The other one, from the Annie Bartholomew fire, was so poor it's gone off for special enhancement. We've a copy here, but it's useless.'

'Mm.' Montgomery was only just listening. His attention had been caught by the appearance of two boys loitering on the fringes of the activity. One was tall, the other younger and shorter. 'Who looked at this film before?' he demanded.

'Grange.'

'And he identified Jordan Hardwick – right? But he's never met Glenn Foley . . .' Deftly he froze the frame and stabbed at the screen with his finger. 'Who do you reckon that is, Will?'

William Bird stared long and hard before he spoke. 'It's Glenn.'

132

16

'I thought Glenn went home at ten thirty,' protested Smythe the next morning. 'His mother confirmed that, didn't she?'

'It's Glenn on the video with Jordan Hardwick,' stated Montgomery, 'and that portion is timed at 00.25 a.m. Just because they were watching the fire doesn't mean they started it, but Glenn certainly has some explaining to do.'

'Especially if the cause of his limp isn't a twisted ankle,' added William Bird.

Jackson listened carefully. 'I don't suppose you're so interested in Crabbe's mistress now,' he said to Montgomery.

'Of course I am. Crabbe is still inexplicably missing, and our body has yet to be identified. Anyone who knows him well must be seen. Have you tracked her down yet?'

'Yeah. I tried that number again yesterday, and this time an answerphone came on. It's the private residence of a man called Mostyn Ellery. He appeared in the golf club list, and a little discreet digging revealed that he's a company executive in his fifties with a youngish American wife called Shona . . . that's the woman's name Andrew gave us . . .'

Behind him, Grange answered a telephone call, and his heavy face lit up. 'Excuse me,' he said as soon as the receiver was replaced. 'That was Professor Frobisher at the hospital. They've got some news about the corpse . . .'

The bank of X-ray boxes shone with soulless, pristine light. Here on the films displayed for the three detectives flesh, blood and bone were reduced to two dimensions, impersonal images in black and white. Selected portions of anatomy for discussion.

Even Montgomery could recognize that these were X-rays of

a skull, although the orientation of one seemed somewhat angled, as if the radiographer had been peering up the subject's nose. The teeth were consequently indistinct, but the eye sockets and other facial structures above were more clearly delineated. Another film alongside seemed to concentrate particularly on the area between the eyes . . .

'These are Robert McPherson's ENT films from 1981,' said the consultant radiologist whom Frobisher had introduced as Dr Lyness. 'He'd had symptoms of sinusitis for some months, and you'll see that the maxillary sinus *here* is opaque, as is the homolateral nasal cavity . . . There was also a history of headaches, and so this film of the frontal and ethmoid sinuses was taken.'

'Could you just orientate us, please?' asked Sergeant Bird. 'These are the eye sockets?'

'The orbits, yes. Ethmoids here, just at the top of the nose. But it's the frontal sinuses we're interested in.' He indicated two billowing translucent areas immediately above the orbits, with scalloped edges which reminded William Bird of the petals of a flower.

'They're asymmetrical,' noted Montgomery.

'The majority are. They're also highly individual. People's frontal sinuses develop during childhood; some remain rudimentary, others are quite florid like these.'

'The point is,' said Frobisher, sliding another film out of a flat brown package, 'these X-rays are almost as useful as a fingerprint.' He thrust the new film under the flanges at the top of the viewing box. 'We took this one from the corpse: same projection, same magnification . . . There were difficulties of interpretation elsewhere in the skull due to the fire damage, but – can you see the similarities?' They could. 'Now look,' he said, superimposing the film over the second film Dr Lyness had discussed.

The scalloped sinuses blended into a single entity; it was a powerful demonstration.

Frobisher was gratified by the detectives' rapt response. 'The body is that of Robert McPherson,' he told them. 'You may be confident of that.'

*

Once again Montgomery found that his quarry was a boy returning home from school. It was far better for Glenn to be questioned in a quiet environment, away from the speculation of classmates and anxieties of the staff. If he was indeed guilty of serial arson, they would all find out soon enough – and Kathleen Foley stood to suffer even more than her son.

'Here comes Glenn,' said William Bird, peering from the car. 'He's on his own.'

Certainly the boy walked with a faint lopsidedness. He limped dejectedly up the path, then vanished round the side of the garage.

'Let's give him a few minutes to settle down,' said Montgomery.

When they did ring the door bell, he sensed a flicker of curtain in an upstairs room even as Kathleen Foley was bustling through the hall.

'May we speak to Glenn, please?' asked Sergeant Bird in his mellow, reassuring voice.

'I – yes, of course. Come inside.' From the living-room they heard her mount the stairs and tap on a door. She called her son's name, then tapped again. Sporadic muffled sounds followed before she reappeared. 'I'm dreadfully sorry,' she gasped. 'Glenn seems to have gone. His bedroom window is open.'

'You're sure he's not hiding upstairs?' asked Montgomery.

'Positive. And we would have seen him if he'd come through the hall . . .'

'Will, the front. I'll take the back garden.' Montgomery ran through the kitchen to the rear of the house and appraised the rectangular garden. It was tidily surrounded by panels of cedar fencing, with no obvious exit except a gate beyond the garage leading straight to Sergeant Bird. If the boy *had* climbed over the fence, which part would he have chosen?

A compost heap in the bottom corner, half hidden behind a small pergola, seemed the most promising area to check.

135

Montgomery clambered on to its springy surface and peered into the neighbouring property; a glimpse of blue behind a flowering currant bush confirmed his reasoning; with a bound he was over and hurtling towards Glenn. The boy didn't try to run any more. He cowered, his face taut with fear, as Montgomery drew up alongside. 'Running away never solved anything,' Montgomery told him, 'but talking might.'

'I – I didn't mean it. I – I shouldn't have done it. I know I shouldn't.' His lip quivered uncontrollably, and he gulped. 'Mum's going to be so mad with me.'

'Let's go back, then we can talk about this properly.' Montgomery maintained a light grip on Glenn's elbow as they walked up the side of the neighbour's house and out into Fielding Avenue. He signalled to William Bird, who was checking front gardens further up the road, and soon they were once more in Kathleen Foley's living-room.

'Do you need my husband?' she asked, glancing nervously at Glenn. 'I'm afraid he's going to be late home tonight.'

'It's all right.' Montgomery suspected Glenn would be more forthcoming in the absence of his father. 'Now, Glenn, we just want to ask you a few questions. You bought some burns dressings yesterday in Green Triangle Pharmacy. Who were they for?'

'Roger.'

'Roger Pearce?'

'That's right. He had an accident with his chemistry set . . .' He broke off as Montgomery slowly shook his head.

'I put it to you, Glenn, that the dressings were for yourself. For your leg, to be precise. I further suggest that the burns were sustained on Saturday night when you set alight the abandoned garage on Hope Street.'

'It's true, isn't it, Glenn?' Sergeant Bird added gently.

The boy gave a jerky nod before glancing at his mother's appalled face. He swallowed convulsively. 'Yes,' he rasped.

'May we see your leg?'

Without a word he rolled his right trouser leg up above the

knee. A bandage was wrapped around the calf; he unwound it to reveal two stained squares of melolin secured by tape. He paused, glanced again at his mother, then ripped off the dressing in one quick movement.

'Oh, Glenn!' cried Kathleen Foley.

The outside of his calf was raw and oozing over an area almost five inches long. 'I splashed the paraffin,' he whispered. 'Suddenly I was on fire.'

His mother was stricken.

'What did you do?' asked Montgomery.

'Someone I was with beat out the flames with a rag.'

'Jordan Hardwick?'

Glenn hesitated.

'We know about Jordan. We have you on film together . . .'

While Mrs Foley redressed the leg, Glenn haltingly explained. 'I had to do it as a sort of test,' he said. 'We knew no one worked in that building any more, so we didn't think it would do any harm . . . Jordan said even if someone owned it there'd be insurance.'

'Did you always try to pick on abandoned buildings?'

Glenn looked up, startled. 'Always?'

'The previous fires. The houses, the shed, the factory . . .'

'That wasn't us. We'd never done it before.'

'You mean there's been a series of fires, and you have admitted to causing the last one, but you deny any connection with the previous events?'

'Yes!'

Montgomery leaned forward. 'Glenn . . . how do you explain the fact that the fire brigade video taken on the night of the blaze at Furlong End Pharmacy shows you and Jordan Hardwick standing at the scene at half-past twelve?'

'Inspector.' Kathleen Foley looked gaunt. 'I'm sorry to interrupt, but that's impossible. Glenn was home before eleven. We spoke about this before.'

'I think we've seen how Glenn is able to leave the house at will,' replied Montgomery. Turning back to the boy, he went on, 'Three nights ago you started a fire in Hope Street. One

137

week before that you were present at a fire here in Furlong End. Wouldn't it be reasonable for people to assume you also started that one?'

'But we didn't!' Glenn was gabbling in his earnestness. 'Jordan told me to come back when I'd said goodnight to my parents – it was another test; he knew I could climb out of the window. He said we'd discuss the challenges he was going to set – just the two of us. I had to pass them to be in the gang. We were walking round the streets about midnight when we realized the chemist's was on fire – flames were shooting into the sky. We stood and watched as the firemen tried to control the blaze, but they didn't have a chance. It was scary and exciting. We didn't know there was anyone inside . . .

'Jordan turned to me, and he said, "That's what you're going to do." And I thought, yes, I can manage that. So a week later, I did . . .'

Jackson stretched at the desk. 'I'm for home,' he announced to Smythe. 'You can leave that blasted telephone; we aren't on "lates" tonight.'

Smythe was constitutionally incapable of ignoring a ringing phone. He lifted the receiver, identified himself to the caller, then listened with an expression of increasing concern. 'You'd better take this,' he hissed to Jackson. 'It's Andrew Dunster again, and he's really upset!'

Jackson gave a muffled snort of annoyance, but accepted the receiver. Andrew probably resented the appearance of Drugs Squad officers at Morgifts. What did the cretin expect?

'Andrew,' he said flatly.

'Sergeant Jackson . . . I'm glad I've caught you. It's Sean – he's gone off his rocker. I think he plans to murder Geoff, make it look like an OD. I'm sure he does!'

'Calm down, Andrew. I thought Sean didn't know Geoff's whereabouts.'

'That's what he *said*. But Geoff must have phoned him when I wasn't around, because yesterday he talked about taking

Geoff some supplies. I guessed he meant Dikes. I asked where Geoff was, because Monica has been frantic; Sean wouldn't say.

'This morning he came in looking really pale and sick. Said he'd got some bad dope from somewhere. Then he said if Geoff was found he'd implicate us both and we'd go down with him. He commented it was better for everyone if Geoff wasn't found . . . I couldn't believe what I was hearing. Sean's known Geoff for years. But his eyes were black and – inhuman, dead, like a shark's eyes. I was bloody terrified.' Andrew's voice came over the line as a wavering falsetto, close to hysteria. 'I tried to laugh it off. I said, "What do you propose, then?" and he flicked this packet in front of my face and said, "I'll give him some of these. He's desperate for a hit. That'll sort him out."

'This afternoon I tried again to find out where Geoff is lying up, but Sean wouldn't drop so much as a hint. I said to him, "You don't need to kill Geoff," and he gave this horrible snicker and said, "Don't worry, Andy baby, he'll carry out the entire execution himself. Just make sure you're with people tonight." '

'Andrew, are you certain he didn't give any kind of clue about Geoff's location? Is he in a house, on a boat – what?'

'I'm sorry. Sean told me nothing at all.'

'And where is Sean now?'

'He's just left the barn.'

17

'What a nightmare,' said Sergeant Bird as Montgomery recounted the substance of Jackson's urgent call. 'If Sean gets to Crabbe before we do, we're never going to find out what really happened.'

Montgomery was already stabbing digits on his mobile

phone. Grim-faced, he waited for several rings before a rich transatlantic female voice came on to the line. The voice quickly lost its warmth when he stated his identity and business.

'Geoff Crabbe? I'm sorry, I don't know anyone of that name. You must have got the wrong number.'

'Mr Crabbe is a member of the same golf club as your husband. We know you've met him several times – the party on New Year's Eve, for instance, when you danced together.'

'Oh, *that* Geoff. Yes, his name *is* Crabbe; I remember now. But I hardly know him.'

'Mrs Ellery . . . I'm afraid I haven't got time to pussyfoot around. We have reason to believe that Geoff is in danger from one of his business associates – acute physical danger. We need to find him urgently. We've exhausted all other possible avenues; you're the only person who can help us.'

There was a shocked silence. 'Danger?' she repeated hesitantly.

'Yes. We think someone wants to kill him. Have you any idea at all where he might be now?'

'I – I haven't seen him in over a week. Listen, Inspector, my husband will be coming home soon. I'm fixing his dinner right now. I don't know anything that will help Geoff, and I really can't talk any more. I'm sorry.'

Tension tore at Montgomery's innards. He had no other leads. He was satisfied that Monica knew nothing, which left only Andrew and Sean. 'I'm sorry, too,' he said, 'but we do require your assistance. I need to meet you now, either at your home or another venue.'

Her voice rose in a wail. 'You *mustn't* come here! You've no right to ruin my life!'

'Suggest somewhere else.'

He heard her swallow. 'Okay . . . okay. I'll leave a note for Mostyn, say one of my girlfriends has got a crisis . . . I'll be at Torvill Park, on a bench overlooking the lake, in fifteen minutes. I'm wearing navy and white.'

When he saw Shona Ellery, Montgomery was struck by her

140

resemblance to Theresa. She had the same wavy black hair, the ice-blue eyes, the pale yet full lips. People were often consistent in their attraction to certain phenotypes, he had found, and Monica, the apparent exception to Geoff's rule, was not a natural blonde.

Shona was immaculately clad in a crisp linen thigh-length dress; the deep V-neck was framed by prominent revers, white slashed with navy. She would certainly be a desirable ornament on the arm of her ageing husband, thought Montgomery as he introduced himself. Without delay he steamed through her weak denials of an affair, and within minutes she was explaining to them the evolution of her relationship with Geoff.

'Mostyn's friends are all so stuffy,' she lamented. 'They're like caricatures – especially together in a pack. Geoff is different; he knows how to loosen up, have fun . . . I feel so much more on his wavelength. It was easy to start an affair with him. Mostyn's often away for a week at a time . . .' She caught Montgomery's look of disapproval, and added hastily, 'Oh no, Geoff never comes to the house. We go to a hotel, or sometimes the cottage.'

'Cottage?'

'It's a little weekend place near Spalding that Mostyn and I have had for years. It belonged to an aunt of his, and she willed it to him before she died. He hardly goes there himself now, though. It's a bit primitive, and there isn't much to do or look at once the bulb season's over.'

Ideal for lovers' trysts, thought Montgomery. *And* escapees from the law. 'Could Geoff be there now?' he asked. 'Does he have a key?'

'Well . . . yes . . . but – what *is* all this? Why is he in trouble? Why is someone after him?'

'Mrs Ellery, I'm sorry, but time is ticking away. Tell me exactly when you last saw Geoff.'

'Sunday morning. Not last Sunday, the week before. We'd spent Saturday night together.'

'At the cottage?' Montgomery kept his tone light,

testing her trustworthiness. Spalding was at least an hour away by car, and Crabbe was unlikely to have met her at midnight.

'No. A hotel in Nottingham.'

'What time was your rendezvous?'

'We met in the bar seven thirty, eight o'clock . . . We had a light supper and went up to our room.'

'Did Geoff stay in your company for the entire evening?' To his annoyance, Montgomery could hear the tightness in his voice. The answer to this question was vital, and Shona was looking at him appraisingly.

'I guess so,' she answered.

'You're sure he didn't leave for any reason after your meal?'

'He didn't leave.'

'What was his manner like that Saturday?'

She shrugged; her mouth curved to form a smile hinting at delicious secrets. 'Same as usual,' she said.

'He wasn't on edge, distracted?'

'Not then.'

'When was he . . .' Montgomery caught sight of William Bird tapping his watch-face and aborted the question. 'Does the cottage have a telephone?' he demanded.

'No. Mostyn is there so seldom, it wasn't worth the rental. He has his mobile, of course – as does Geoff.'

'Do you know Geoff's number?'

Sergeant Bird assumed the role of amanuensis as Shona Ellery drawled a series of digits. The combination tallied with that volunteered by Monica days earlier – a number no one ever answered . . .

'Can you lend us a key to the cottage, Mrs Ellery?'

'Well . . .'

'We want to avoid damage.'

'Oh . . . There's only the main key. Geoff has the spare.' She bit her lower lip and blood flared beneath the surface. 'I – I would have to go home. Mostyn might be there by now . . .'

'I'm sure you'll think of some excuse,' said Montgomery coolly.

142

The Sierra sped eastwards along the A52, past green fields basking in the clear light of evening. As Grantham receded with the slowly sinking sun, the landscape became flatter, and soon the dykes and drains of Lincolnshire's fenlands began to appear. Montgomery was anxious; Shona Ellery had given him complex directions to the cottage, and admitted that it was difficult to find. Only occasional church spires served as landmarks on the near-treeless horizon.

'Pity we're just too late for the tulips,' said Sergeant Bird by his side. 'You'll be passing the bulbfields soon – it looks just like Holland here in April and early May. The soil is reclaimed marshland – full of nutrients.'

'Mm.'

'Our family used to go to the Spalding Bulb Festival every year when I was a lad. There were all these elaborate floats covered with flowers – vivid colour everywhere.' He gave a contented sigh, confirmed a navigatory query for Montgomery, was silent for some minutes, then sniffed the air. 'Smell that?' he said. 'Marshes; saltings. We're getting near The Wash.' He pointed ahead through the windscreen. 'Somewhere out there over the water is Hunstanton, the only East Anglian coastal town to face due west.'

'I can cap that,' murmured Montgomery. 'There's a place in Canada where you can look north and see America. At Windsor, Ontario, a tongue of Canadian land swings beneath Detroit . . . Now, Will . . . here's the post office she mentioned. Final bastion of human habitation . . . field of cows on the right – yes . . . lane bends sharply . . . deserted cottage – yes . . . another one on the horizon.' He pulled off the road and stopped the car alongside the empty cottage. 'Any closer and we'll be seen.' He peered down the rough track which stretched between the two ramshackle buildings. It ran along the top of a four-foot dyke, exposed for miles around. 'I can't see any silver Granada.' There had been an APB out for some days on Geoff's car, to no avail. 'No white Capri, either.'

Andrew had been unable to offer Jackson any details of Sean's number plate.

'They could be hidden, sir – which is more than we shall be if we start walking along the top of this dyke. What do you suggest?'

Montgomery compressed his lips. 'We've got three options. We try to approach unobserved by floundering through the marsh, we lose another hour by waiting till dark, or we walk up to the cottage openly in as unthreatening a manner as we can assume. Personally, I prefer the third.'

'And the local force . . . ?'

'No. Time's too short, and we can't risk them arriving mob-handed. We don't even know if Crabbe is here. Are you ready, Will?' He left the shadow of the cottage wall and began a leisurely stride down the long track towards the isolated building on the near horizon. 'Try to avoid looking like John Wayne,' he hissed as William Bird marched along in step at his right elbow.

'You said Sean had a Bowie knife,' murmured the sergeant. 'What about Crabbe himself? Any chance of a firearm?'

'That never used to be his style, but things change. Even petty crooks tool themselves up these days . . . damn it, this track must be half a mile or more.' He increased his pace and soon the tangy whiff of the sea was stronger than ever. The weathered cottage loomed before them; there were curtains at the windows, but no peering faces.

'There's a kind of lean-to garage on the other side,' said William Bird.

'Let's try and sneak a look before we knock.' Montgomery once more scanned the empty windows, then ducked round the back of the cottage. There were no signs of life as they passed the kitchen and came to the rear of the garage. To Montgomery's disappointment there was no door, but a narrow row of grubby windows beckoned high in the wall just beneath the guttering pipe. 'First floor, please,' he whispered; William Bird obligingly facilitated the leg-up. 'Silver Granada!' Montgomery was hugely relieved.

Their detective work had paid off . . . but where was Geoff Crabbe?

Back on *terra* reasonably *firma*, Montgomery led the way round to the front of the house. The light was fading now; a seabird mewed mournfully and a faint onshore breeze carried the suggestion of dank mudflats. He glanced into the window of a small sitting-room and pulled up sharply, his heart thudding. Inside, on a low pink couch, reposed two feet attached to an as yet invisible body. They wore socks, but no shoes.

Wordlessly, Montgomery gestured to Sergeant Bird and craned to see more. The owner of the feet was a man, clad in slacks and a dark green shirt, and his knees were drawn up as if he was in agony, and a gold watch glinted at his wrist, and – yes! The contorted face was that of Geoff Crabbe . . .

'Looks as if we've come too late,' said William Bird with a sigh.

'Not necessarily.' Montgomery felt anger boiling inside him, anger against Sean Turner and something more diffuse which he could not identify. He stared again at the body, focusing intently on the colour of the exposed flesh. The room was full of shadows, but the skin could nevertheless be evaluated. It was an unpleasant, sickly white.

With a drained, sick feeling of his own, Montgomery turned away from the window and fumbled in his pocket for the key.

'Sir!' Behind him, William Bird gave an excited gasp. 'The legs just moved!'

Montgomery swung round and peered through the glass. The legs did indeed twitch; a faint groan reached his ears.

He knocked on the window, and Geoff Crabbe's eyes flew open. For a moment he seemed confused, then he raised himself blinking to a sitting position. He looked at them; an expression of alarm was swiftly followed by a grimace of pain.

'Are you all right?' yelled Montgomery. 'Stay there; we'll come and help you.' He used the key that Shona had given

145

him and gained the tiny entrance hall just as Geoff Crabbe was staggering from the room.

'Don't come any nearer,' said Crabbe hoarsely. He crouched forward, holding his stomach with his left arm, teeth clenched.

'We thought you might need medical help.'

'Sure you did. And I'm the president of Bolivia.' He kept his right arm concealed. 'I know what you want. You want to pin that fire on me – and the death of that geezer McPherson. Give a dog a bad name: that's the way you people operate. And there's plenty of circumstantial evidence, so you're home and dry. Saves you doing any real detecting, doesn't it? Keeps the figures looking good, keeps the taxpayer happy . . .'

Montgomery ignored the gibes. 'Why are you here, Geoff?' he asked. 'If you're so anxious about circumstantial evidence, was it wise to disappear like this?'

'I'm treasure hunting,' he leered.

'Treasure?'

'Wicked King John. Lost the Crown Jewels in The Wash when his baggage train got bogged down. He didn't quite have Moses's way with water . . .' He giggled hebephrenically, but the laugh was cut short by a spasm of agony.

'Geoff, you're ill. What's wrong?'

'Dunno. Something I ate, perhaps.'

'Has Sean been here? Has he given you drugs?'

Crabbe's sunken eyes momentarily glinted as he flicked an assessing glance at Montgomery. 'Sean's never been here,' he said.

'You're sure? We have information that he was planning to bring you impure drugs which could be lethal.'

Now Crabbe was staring at him intently.

'We came to warn you,' went on Montgomery. 'If you've taken something –'

'I haven't,' interrupted Crabbe. 'I've got cramps, that's all. Something I ate. I told you . . .'

'Turkey,' said William Bird quietly in the background.

'Cold turkey,' agreed Montgomery. Withdrawal symptoms:

146

Geoff was missing his Diconal. 'Ring for some medical assistance, Will.'

'No.' Crabbe's voice was suddenly strong. 'Don't do that,' he said. Slowly he brought into view the arm he had been keeping hidden and raised it to waist height. There in his hand was a large pistol, the barrel pointing straight at Montgomery.

18

'Don't be a fool,' said Montgomery wearily. 'Put that down.' He wasn't sure if the weapon was genuine, but had to work on that assumption.

'Who's the fool, Mr Montgomery? You, if you think I'm going to let you fit me up.'

'You know me better than that.'

'All right – maybe not you personally, but the rest of your crowd. Well, I'm not playing ball. Come in here, and keep your hands where I can see them.' He gestured with the gun towards the sitting-room, and the two detectives trooped through the doorway. The room was dim in the absence of artificial illumination; outside beyond the window the green of the flat fields was obscured by a translucent veil of ground mist.

Montgomery strolled to the centre of the room as Crabbe took up residence once more on the couch. 'You still haven't answered my question,' he said. 'Why *are* you here, incommunicado? Monica has been worried out of her mind.'

Crabbe's face hardened. 'Now I know you're lying,' he said. 'Monica is well aware that I'm okay.'

'You've spoken to her yourself?'

'Not directly. But I sent a message.'

'Via whom? Sean, by any chance?'

Crabbe said nothing.

'Monica never got any message. She's genuinely afraid for you – though she's torn between wanting to discuss it with me and insisting hollowly that you've been going straight. Ring her now; if your mobile's discharged you can borrow mine.'

Doubts ebbed and flowed behind Crabbe's eyes. He looked weak and ill, with a flat pallor and a thin sheen of perspiration just above his upper lip. Montgomery judged the distance between them and knew that he had a ninety-five per cent chance of kicking the pistol out of Geoff's grasp. It would be preferable, however, for Geoff to hand it over voluntarily.

'Andrew thinks Sean is afraid you'll implicate them,' Montgomery continued. 'But I'd go one further. I reckon Sean has his own agenda. He wants your cake, Geoff, and he wants you out of the way.'

As Geoff frowned, struggling with the concept, Sergeant Bird cleared his throat. 'Excuse me,' he said from his post near the window. 'Loath as I am to interrupt, I think you should know that there's a white Capri on the dyke road, heading this way.'

Montgomery looked directly at Geoff Crabbe, then held out his hand, palm upwards. 'Come on, Geoff. He's not bringing you groceries, is he? Don't make this mess any worse.'

Crabbe hesitated, then slowly offered up the pistol. 'It's a replica,' he said. 'I don't believe in firearms.'

Montgomery briskly confirmed the status of the weapon, and shut it in a nearby drawer. 'Act naturally,' he said to Geoff. 'Sergeant Bird and I will conceal ourselves on the premises.'

That proved to be easier said than done. In the end, William Bird retreated to the bedroom while Montgomery curled up behind the couch. The Capri passed the window, its engine note aggressive, and swung off the track to park beyond the cottage. They heard the slam of the car door; seconds later there was a tapping at the front of the house.

148

From his cramped position, Montgomery heard Geoff drag himself to the hall to admit Sean. 'Christ!' said that worthy, striding into the sitting-room. 'What a dump in the back of beyond! I've been lost for hours on these frigging roads. Thought I was going to end up in Norwich. I've brought you the gear you asked for; you look as though you need it now.'

There was a rustling sound as Geoff unwrapped and inspected the gear. 'These look different,' he said. 'Not the usual colour.'

'Different make, but they're better. Trust me. I've had some myself.'

'Thanks, Sean. You're a pal. How is Monica?'

'Doing fine. The police are hassling her a bit, but she only knows what I tell her.'

'You gave her the message?'

'Yeah. I said some trouble had blown up with a deal in Bulgaria and you'd gone to sort it out personally. I said you'd be in touch as soon as you could.'

'Good. She knows I keep my passport at the barn. What about the police?'

'They're still sniffing round the barn. You need to lie low a bit yet, until they get bored . . . here, have some of these now I've brought them.'

'In a minute. Do you want some tea?'

'Got any lager?'

'None left. It's tea or nothing.'

'Forget it. Hey, listen, Geoff . . . did you know that guy was still inside when you fired the building? You never told us what went wrong. Did he try and blackmail you?' His voice sounded ghoulishly excited.

There was silence, then a sigh. 'I've told you, I wasn't involved. Not that the police will believe me.'

'Get out of it, Geoff. This is Sean you're talking to. I don't care about McPherson – he had it coming. Whatever you did is cool by me . . .'

A sharp creak overhead axed his blandishments.

149

'What was that?' demanded Sean after a pause. 'Is someone else here? Is it Shona?'

'Nobody. This bleedin' cottage is full of noises.'

'Don't talk bilge. That was a floorboard. What are you hiding?' His voice was tense now with alarm. 'Is it cops? For God's sake! I'm out of here!'

Montgomery rocketed to his feet as Sean blundered through the hall. Geoff was leaning shakily against the wall by the window. 'He took the drugs,' he said. 'He'll destroy them.'

Even as William Bird thundered down the narrow staircase, Montgomery was out on the dyke track, sprinting towards the Capri. In his haste Sean tried to insert the wrong key then, baulked and agitated, dropped the bunch. Montgomery caught him up and seized his arm, but before he could secure his grip Sean had squirmed free and attempted a crashing head-butt. Just in time Montgomery jerked his face away, but a glancing blow on the temple left him dazed. In the gathering gloom he saw Sean's wiry form snaking back the way he had come, past the front of the cottage towards the waiting bulk of Sergeant Bird.

Sean flung his arm aloft, fingers splayed: a small package spiralled into the air over the marsh and vanished behind a grassy tussock. Then he pulled something from his waistband – the Bowie knife. William Bird took up a defensive stance in Sean's line of escape, and a confusion of feints and lunges followed before they grappled at close quarters. There was a grunt of pain from Sean and the knife fell to the ground. Moments later the antagonists were scrabbling on the dirt track, rolling ever closer to the edge of the dyke.

Montgomery cleared his brain and began to lope towards the shadowy tangle of limbs. He was anxious about his colleague: William Bird was not the fittest of men, and who knew what else Sean might have hidden about his person?

With a startled yell, William Bird vanished over the edge, pulling Sean with him. There was a muted splash as they hit the soggy field below, and continued wrestling with each other. Then Montgomery heard a grunt. Moments later Sean slithered over the lip of the dyke. He knelt on the track, lungs heaving, tugged his ankle away from Sergeant Bird's grasping hand, then pounced on the abandoned knife. His face twisted with hate, he swung towards Montgomery. 'Come and get it, Mr Detective,' he hissed.

'*Sean!*' The shout powered from the cottage doorway. 'Drop the knife!'

Sean turned with an expletive on his lips. Fifteen feet away, Geoff Crabbe had summoned the last of his strength. As he stood glaring at his sidekick, the dark shape of the pistol in his raised hands was unmistakable.

People greeted the dawn chorus with a variety of emotions. For some, it simply represented a joyous start to the coming day. For others – exhausted new mothers, resident hospital doctors, insomniacs – the swell of cheeps and twitters took on a mocking tone.

Montgomery rolled out of his bed and gave up trying to sleep. He felt dry-eyed and achy, and suspected that Sean Turner, festering in the discomfort of a police cell, had spent a similarly poor night. Geoff Crabbe, in hospital under supervision, had probably fared better.

Nagging anxieties had plagued Montgomery ever since the action of the previous evening had subsided. Anxieties, and mental images: Sergeant Bird muddily retrieving the incriminating packet, the handcuffed Sean Turner's palpable loathing of all three individuals in his company – and Geoff Crabbe's utterance as he handed back the replica pistol. 'I'm trusting you, Mr Montgomery,' he had said in a low voice, his face drawn with pain and fatigue. 'Don't let me down.'

Montgomery sat on the side of the bed, his shoulders slumped. His brief was not to let down Robert McPherson, or Theresa, or Honour. There was a nasty, bullying core to Geoff Crabbe's personality, yet was he actually capable of cold-blooded murder? Sean had apparently thought so. Many of his actions had been governed by an assumption of Geoff's

151

guilt. But was Sean merely attributing to someone else his own capacity for viciousness? Geoff's replies to Sean's eager questions were meaningless; he had known that Montgomery was concealed behind the couch.

No, the crunch had come if anything a little too soon. Montgomery had been unable to marshal any direct evidence against Geoff. No one had *seen* him near the pharmacy on that Saturday night, though several people knew of his ten o'clock appointment. And now Shona Ellery was claiming to have been with him at the crucial time.

There were other mysteries, too. Glenn Foley still swore that he saw Robert McPherson leave the pharmacy at ten thirty and walk up towards the car-park. In view of Glenn's own admission of arson at the Hope Street garage, one could be cynical about his statement, dismissing it as an attempt to evade responsibility for any part of the harm which had befallen the pharmacist. But two things stood against that interpretation. Firstly, Glenn's attitudes at interview had been entirely consistent with his admitted level of involvement. The first time he had been merely wary, the second time frankly terrified. Secondly, and more important, Grange had unearthed another witness who noticed a man with spectacles answering Robert McPherson's description leaving the pharmacy at ten thirty.

If this were true, what had Geoff Crabbe been doing at the time? It didn't make sense, and the more Montgomery tried to force Geoff Crabbe into this misshapen frame, the more his gut instincts told him that the real answer lay elsewhere . . .

He stretched, and padded to the bathroom for a shower followed by a careful shave, leaving Carole asleep. Pulling on casual clothes, he quietly descended to the kitchen, poured himself a glass of orange juice and slipped out into the back garden.

It was cool beneath the willow tree. The birdsong was less intrusive now, and the grey dawn light had brightened into soft mother of pearl. The day promised to be full of sunshine. Sunshine for some, at any rate.

He turned and saw Carole stepping barefoot towards him through the grass. She wore a short dressing-gown and a conspiratorial smile.

'I'm sorry,' he said humbly. 'I didn't mean to wake you.'

'Let me make you some breakfast,' she said. 'You'll need it today. How about bacon and tomato?' She knew he was not fond of eggs early in the morning.

'Justin will smell that. He'll be down like a shot.'

'No, he won't He's comatose right now. So is Heather.'

Montgomery wandered through to the living-room while the scent of frying bacon gathered strength. He pulled back the curtains and idly straightened a cushion. *Lord of the Flies* lay on a nearby miniature coffee table; he picked up the book, ruefully acknowledging that he had actually been enjoying the story and would now be unlikely to finish it for some time.

Removing his bookmark, he glanced at the page to refresh his memory. Ah, yes . . . the conflict he had predicted had indeed ignited. Members of the two factions had just fought violently for possession of Piggy's precious spectacles, and Piggy was now bereft . . .

His gaze wandered to the start of the new chapter. '. . . Piggy sat expressionless behind the luminous wall of his myopia.' Poor boy. Montgomery himself had near-perfect vision, but he could try to imagine the breadth of the handicap for someone else, especially in a hostile environment.

He closed the book, then paused. 'That's wrong,' he said aloud.

'What's wrong?' Carole was leaning round the door lintel, a fork in her hand.

'This book. There's a scientific inaccuracy . . . You remember the boy Piggy? The other castaways have been using his spectacles to light fires on the island, but it turns out he's short-sighted.'

'Why is that a problem?'

'Spectacles for myopes *diverge* the sun's rays rather than concentrating them. You'd never get a fire to light that way in a million years.' He followed her back into the kitchen. 'I thought you said Golding had the Nobel Prize.'

'For Literature, not Physics.' Carole speared cooked rashers of bacon with the fork and transferred them to a plate. 'Anyway, did he actually specify myopia?'

'Yes. Near the end of the book. There were hints before, but my mind was on other ramifications.' He took the plate to the table and sat down, but paused with the cutlery in his hands. 'My God!' he whispered softly.

'Richard?'

'Surely . . . yes! That really could be . . . That's why – yes . . .'

'What are you talking about?'

He sat a few seconds more, dazed, then stood up clumsily. 'I'm sorry, I must go right now. I need to check on something for the McPherson case. It's vital – those men we arrested last night may be innocent.'

'Please eat. You don't know when you'll next have a chance.'

He took two mouthfuls to please her, washed them down with coffee, then ran for the stairs. He cleaned his teeth, changed into a lightweight navy suit, kissed his wife and hurried out to the Sierra. It was not yet six thirty.

Carole halted him with a signal just as he was preparing to reverse down the drive. 'There was no chance to tell you yesterday,' she said through the open car window, 'but that ceramics book I was waiting for came back to the library. It lists all the British manufacturers' marks. Your little porcelain cup was made by the firm of Thomas Pringle in Stoke-on-Trent, and the design was registered in 1965. I suppose we could have tried to contact the Patent Office in London, but I doubt it would have been any quicker. Might that date be important?'

Montgomery made a swift mental calculation. 'Very,' he said.

He drove steadily north-east along the A612 towards Southwell. The road was almost empty at that hour, and only required the concentration necessary to negotiate its rural pere-grinations. Montgomery's brain was largely free to analyse his theory. He ran a mental checklist of the more bizarre, unanswered facts of the case; the theory fitted, but as yet there was no real evidence. He hoped to find some imminently.

As the Sierra crested the rise overlooking Southwell, the Minster glowed before him in the weak early sunshine like a pastel painting. He wanted to stop right there, to feel, to understand, but time was too short. Instead he motored through the twisting streets of the town, past the russet houses to a destination beyond . . .

Montgomery spent ten minutes with grass beneath his feet; no one came near him, no one even saw him. Then he climbed back into the car and made his way to police headquarters. In his office he sat thinking, head in hands, then sighed and walked round to the small room where the video monitors were. He checked the cassettes without much hope, then paused with a murmur of thanksgiving: the promised copy of a particular fire brigade video *had* arrived.

He fed the cassette into the slot and watched, trying to orien-tate himself as hazy images of men and women flickered in the reflected glow from the fire. This was *his* fire, the one in which Annie Bartholomew had nearly died, and even this sterile, two-dimensional view of the event flooded Montgomery with un-pleasant sensations – the heat, the *noise*, the crawling fear . . .

He watched the film once, and then again. Just when he was resigning himself to failure, something caught his eye. Away from the main group of spectators, alone and intent in the background, was a figure he now recognized.

'Sir?'

'You're early, Will.'

'Are you going to interrogate Sean yourself?'

'No.'

Montgomery's car reprised its earlier journey as the morning continued to brighten. The air was absolutely still; beneath a

155

pellucid sky the fields lay motionless; not a whisper of a breeze rustled the tall trees flanking Southwell Minster. Back at the station, Sean Turner was in the competent hands of Jackson and the Drugs Squad officers. Sergeant Bird, meanwhile, sat sombrely alongside Montgomery as they entered Bramton village, swung past the church and came to a halt in the cul-de-sac of red-brick houses beyond.

Vera Blenkinsop was standing outside her own front gate directing an earnest monologue at a captive friend. Her face lit up as the detectives climbed from the car. 'Sergeant!' she exclaimed. 'How very nice. I was just wondering . . .'

She broke off at the sight of Montgomery's grim expression.

19

'Mrs McPherson . . .' Montgomery's voice was very gentle as Honour opened the door of The Old Rectory in response to their knock. Vera Blenkinsop had been successfully jetti-soned: just the two conservatively dressed detectives met Honour's apprehensive, bespectacled gaze.

'Inspector?' She didn't move; it was as if she knew.

'We've come for the letter. Robert's letter.'

'Ah . . .' She stood back to let them enter, then led them through the hallway, where Alistair and Isabel seemed to look down from their portraits at the intruders. Montgomery glanced at the glass case of possessions as they passed; half hidden in the corner was a silver tray and a delicate porcelain tea set, white patterned with pink roses. The teapot, cups, milk jug and sugar basin were all perfectly shaped, but two-thirds the normal adult size. There were only five cups. 'These were Bella's?' he asked.

Wordless, she nodded. With painfully precise steps she escorted them to the drawing-room, then paused in the doorway. 'Someone told you about Bella?' she asked.

'Someone tried to. But we weren't ready to listen . . . I went to St Michael's churchyard this morning. I saw her grave.'

'Please take a seat,' she said, and left them near the window overlooking the long garden. The room was cool, but outside, the roses and lilac and lavender basked under the sunshine of a perfect English summer's day. William Bird visually sought out the shrubs beyond: the *Berberis* was no longer orange, but the border thicket was flourishing, uncut, branches reaching to ten feet and more. Together, Nature and man had effectively sealed off the past.

Until now . . .

The halting tap of high heels on wood signalled Honour's return. She walked to Montgomery and handed him a white envelope, then retreated to a high-backed chair opposite. Montgomery examined the envelope; it bore a Nottingham postmark dated the Monday morning following the fire. Extracting two sheets of white vellum covered with handwriting, he positioned the letter for Sergeant Bird to read simultaneously.

There was no address or date. 'Dear Mother,' Robert had written, 'we have never been close, and until today I didn't understand why. Now that I do understand, I am filled with horror and shame and sadness. All these years you have protected me from the knowledge of the terrible thing I did. Bella had been wiped from my mind like a name deleted from that magic slate I used to play with. My own sister. But today I found the enclosed cutting among Father's papers in the attic – and suddenly it all came back. Everything. That tea set, my jealousy, the fire – everything . . .'

Montgomery sent an interrogative look towards Honour; silently she held out a fragile, yellowed piece of newsprint. There was a heading, 'Boy Kills Sister in Garden Fire', followed by three paragraphs describing the event. Robert, aged seven, had been 'emulating the gardener' by making a bonfire of garden rubbish. Unfortunately the nearby summer house, where his three-year-old sister Bella had been playing with her dolls, was engulfed and the child perished.

157

Montgomery passed the clipping to Sergeant Bird, and resumed his reading of Robert McPherson's letter. 'As you know so well, Mother, ever since I saw Auntie Isabel's broken body being carried back to the house, I was anxious and emotional. You couldn't bear my clinging, I couldn't bear to be shut out – so I lit fires. Each one gave me a surge of relief, and also the bonus of attention. Even Father's anger was better than being ignored. But it didn't take long for the anxiety to build up again, and I would feel compelled to light another fire. You thought I was just a naughty boy playing with matches, but it was a *need*, something I had to do.

'I remember now that sunny day I killed Bella. I didn't mean her to die, but I did mean to frighten her. Father had given her that delicate tea set, for "when she was a big girl", and I had never received a present so special, chosen by him. I was tense with jealousy and rage, yet you told us to go out and play together. Bella took her dolls, Pansy and Geranium, into the summer house and babbled to them endlessly and poured "tea" from her plastic teapot. I decided to spoil her pleasure, to smoke her out.

'There was a pile of garden waste just behind the summer house, twigs and branches, all tinder-dry in the heat. I dragged them up the side to the front corner and made a bonfire, so the smoke would drift inside the door. Then I lit it, with matches from a box you imagined you'd hidden in the black tea caddy. It crackled, and I was excited, and coils of smoke began to rise into the air.

'Suddenly, there was a flare and the pile shifted. It blocked the lower part of the doorway, and I could see Bella inside, her eyes wide with fright. The summer house itself began to catch fire. Now the crackles were sinister, evil . . . I pulled at the branches and yelled to Bella to come out, but she shrank against the back wall and I was too scared to go inside.

'I remember running to the herb garden where you had been collecting mint, Mother, but you were no longer there. When I found you in the kitchen my throat was so dry I could hardly speak. I remember your look of stark terror when I gasped out a few words, how I couldn't keep up with you as you rushed down the lawn – and the blood-chilling, animal wail as you saw the mass of roaring incandescence that had been the summer house.'

Montgomery paused again, feeling some imprint of the horror touching his spine with shivery fingers. Slowly he raised his gaze to Honour; her face was like a skull.

'We explained to the police that Robert had seen our gardener's occasional bonfires and was trying to be helpful,' she said, instinctively knowing what point in the letter Montgomery had reached. 'We sent Robert away with a family friend for a long holiday in Criccieth; when he came back, all trace of the incident seemed to have been wiped from his mind. And all trace of Bella . . .'

Reluctantly, Montgomery prepared to read the final portion. 'All these years, Mother, I didn't know what I had done. When dark moods were upon me, I thought it was because of poor Auntie Isabel. I could remember her – isn't it strange! – quite distinctly, even though I was so young when she died.

'So I grew up, I bought the shop, I got married, all the while ignorant. I must have thought I could be normal after all. But I wasn't. I couldn't give Theresa affection in the way she craved. No matter how much I tried to overcome my aversion, I found the concept of touch was distasteful to me. Then business went downhill, rivals didn't play by the rules, anxiety was gouging at me again . . . I found myself one night outside an empty house with a bottle of paraffin and some matches in my hand, and I doused a stack of rubbish with the paraffin and watched as the flames gathered strength. It didn't unlock any memories. Instead, I felt an explosion of relief, as if every source of tension was being purged by the fire. A few weeks later, I did it again. And again.

'Last time I started a fire I nearly killed someone. I thought the house was empty, but a woman was rescued at the very last moment. I was sick with remorse, *even while knowing that I would do it again*. I am a danger to people, and always will be.

'Don't curse Father for keeping the newspaper cutting. It

has made everything clear to me. Suddenly a path beckons through the wilderness, and I am grateful. I know what I must do, and I am confident that it is right.

'Don't grieve for me, Mother. All along I have failed – professionally, as a husband, as a brother and son. I am even being blackmailed over matters where I can never prove my innocence. But now I can make amends to you, to Theresa. I shall kill myself painlessly with drugs, though everyone except you will think I died in the fire. The property is insured, as is my life, so Theresa will have some money when I'm gone. I hope she finds happiness with someone else. She deserves it. Try to be kind to her, for my sake.

'Goodbye, then, Mother. I'm so sorry I robbed you of Bella. This afternoon I took one of her little cups from the set in the hall you always told me was Auntie Isabel's. I shall have it with me when I die – something Bella loved.

'Forgive me. Robert.'

Montgomery lowered the pages to his lap and said nothing. Honour stared across the room at the wall opposite with tearless eyes. 'Robert never wrote so freely before,' she said, her voice almost stony. 'If he wrote at all, it was two stiff little lines.'

The first real communication, thought Montgomery: too late. 'Tell us about Bella,' he said.

'Bella . . . she was a dear little girl. I was carrying her when Isabel was alive, though we didn't know the baby's gender then, and Isabel knitted such a lovely matinée jacket in white . . . Isabel's dreadful death almost brought on the birth prematurely, but we managed to struggle to term, and when our daughter was born it was like a consolation, especially for Alistair. We had no hesitation in naming her Bella.

'Perhaps we did favour her above Robert. Or perhaps any sibling would have displeased him. But he never made any attempt to be likeable. He was a sullen, secretive child. Bella, by contrast, had such a sunny disposition. No tantrums, no whining demands . . .

160

'Alistair went to Stoke-on-Trent one day when Bella was three, to help out a friend with some legal matters. The friend was a director of Pringle and Son, a ceramics firm who make limited edition items in fine porcelain. When Alistair saw the tea set, he was terribly keen to have it for Bella, even though she was far too young at that point. She played every day with her plastic set, and he knew she'd love "real" cups with a pink rose pattern.

'So he brought it home, and gave her the present, and told her she could use it when she was a big girl, but she could look at it any time. I can't remember what he brought for Robert; I think it was a toy car.

'Bella asked to see the set every day that week, and I would show it to her and let her hold the little cups. She was enrapt. I noticed that Robert was quiet, but sulking was so normal for him I heard no alarm bells. After a week of Robert hanging around inside on perfectly sunny days, I packed them off down the garden together to play.' Honour's eyelids fluttered and at last she looked directly at Montgomery. 'The rest you now know,' she said.

There was an awkward silence.

'You stayed on here after the tragedy,' observed William Bird.

'Yes . . . our first instinct was to move, to go hundreds of miles away. I never wanted to see the ruins of the summer house again. But this was Alistair's family home, and so much of our identity lay here . . . In the end, we gave the land to Vera and her husband, and we stayed. Vera has been loyal over the years . . . not a word ever reached Robert's ears. But I suppose she had suspicions about this last fire, and told you . . . ?'

'No,' said Montgomery, 'it wasn't Vera. We worked it out.' In his mind, he added, 'With unexpected help from a book.'

'Was it realistic, I wonder,' said Montgomery to Sergeant Bird a few minutes later, 'to expect that the secret could be kept indefinitely from Robert in such a tight-knit community?'

'I think it was.' William Bird paused to close the lych-gate of St Michael's church behind them. 'It's not a topic anyone would want to introduce to a schoolboy, and later he moved closer to the city.'

'But there must have been clues.'

'Indeed – and they didn't register with him. Why should they? He wasn't seeking such information. I know of families where the whole community has been aware of the existence of half-brothers or half-sisters from previous marriages, yet the children involved knew nothing of their extra relatives. These things *can* be kept secret.'

They walked along a gravel path flanked by gravestones. Just ahead were two freshly dug mounds festooned with wreaths, but Montgomery angled away towards the older part of the churchyard, where the grass was longer, more straggly, like the far end of Vera Blenkinsop's garden. 'You know,' he said, 'I felt a peculiar chill down by the fruit trees in Vera's garden. A sudden sense of desolation.'

'So did I,' said his companion. 'Very strongly. I wish I'd known . . . Oh.' Montgomery had stopped by a handsome white marble headstone carved with a kneeling angel in bas-relief. 'Isabel,' it said. 'Always loved, always missed.' Beneath were her full name, the dates of her life and a portion of the Twenty-third Psalm.

'It was easy to find the grave this morning,' Montgomery admitted. 'The stone does rather stand out. But from that point I was only guessing. I checked every headstone from the date of Isabel's death until I came across one with the same surname . . .' He padded through the grass right over to the cemetery wall, ducking under a hanging chestnut bough. The last grave in the row was shorter than the others, with no headstone but a small decorated urn on a grey marble plinth. The tilted front face of the plinth bore the inscription 'Bella McPherson, beloved daughter of Alistair and Honour', with her dates and beneath, 'Suffer the Little Children to Come unto Me.'

The urn was full of marigolds. 'Fresh flowers,' said Sergeant Bird.

'Yes. This is a well-tended grave. Honour must come here frequently. It's only the grass that needs attention.' Montgomery glanced around at nearby epitaphs as a welcome breeze stirred the leaves above him into lazy movement. 'Reunited' was the one he liked best; it gave him hope for the future. 'I wonder where they'll choose to bury Robert?' he said. 'Here, or . . . ?'

'That will be Theresa's decision,' stated William Bird.

20

Robert McPherson's letter crackled in Montgomery's inside pocket as the two detectives left Bramton and drove the short distance to Southwell. They parked in the large car-park opposite the Minster and entered the honey-coloured building by the north porch. Inside, the nave was cool and cavernous; visitors walked softly between the huge Norman pillars, craning their necks to the roof and clerestory arches in silent wonder, or clustered in hushed discussion of the myriad artefacts in stone, glass and wood.

William Bird paused by the Bishop's wooden throne and guiltily ran his finger over the carved coat of arms at the front. The pulpit nearby was even more elaborate, with carved figures round its outer circumference and a canopied roof. He drew Montgomery's attention to one of the figures. 'That's Paulinus, a missionary bishop from York who is thought to have founded a church here about AD 630. There's been a relationship with York ever since, though Southwell got its own bishop in the 1880s. This building is a Minster, a Cathedral and a parish church all rolled into one.'

Alongside the pillar opposite was a tall brass lectern surmounted by an eagle. 'Is that the famous Newstead lectern?' asked Montgomery. 'The one that was found in the pond?'

'No. This is a replica, but the real one stands in the quire, behind that screen.' He pointed up the nave to the triple arched chancel screen with its light, attractive carvings.

Montgomery nodded, and turned with mild regret away from the eastern end of the Minster, from the allure of the carvings in the chancel itself and the octagonal chapter house. Instead, he retraced Robert McPherson's imagined steps, westwards towards the font, to the back row of chairs. Here he had listened to Evensong, to the pure voices of young boys singing a Vaughan Williams anthem. He had sat alone, trying to come to terms with his discovery, seeking God, perhaps, or feeling he was beyond redemption . . . Then the head verger had come along with his keys and Robert had made his bleak progress to Furlong End.

'He couldn't have gone to St Michael's,' murmured William Bird, tuning in telepathically to Montgomery's thoughts as he so often did. 'There might have been friends of his mother's there, still arranging the flowers. He couldn't risk it. Here was the most obvious place.' They stood in silence for a minute, both knowing they were incapable of appreciating the full extent of Robert McPherson's mental turmoil. Then they exited via the south transept and stood in the sunshine by the gothic ruins of the Archbishop's Palace.

'He found the cutting in the attic about three or four o'clock,' mused William Bird. 'He probably did hear Mary Wilsmore ringing the door bell, but he didn't want to answer. He must have felt a need to get out, though, to get away. When he *did* come down, Honour and Vera Blenkinsop were just arriving at the front door. He left abruptly – Vera said he was unusually rude.

'He came here, possibly for some hours, but eventually he had to move on. Perhaps he was still deciding, or perhaps his decision was already made. Either way, he ended up at Furlong End. He had an appointment with Geoff Crabbe over matters which must by now have seemed crashingly irrelevant. All he wanted to do was write his letter and kill himself. So . . .'

'He rang Geoff and postponed the meeting,' said Montgomery.

'As simple as that?'

'Yes. Geoff actually says he was contacted from a phone box early in the evening, so he may have been rung from Southwell. The fact that there would be no record of the call helped to bolster his idea that no one would believe in his innocence.'

'At the pharmacy, Robert wrote to his mother – reams and reams, opening up in a way he never had before. He was convinced that what he was doing was the best for all of them, and he wanted to express his remorse to her in particular. Right into the middle of this blundered Margaret Kendall . . .'

'She was lucky he managed to be civil at all.'

'Yes. When she'd gone – and Judy – there wasn't much left for him to do. He lit a fire down in the stock room, went upstairs, lit another to be sure, then injected himself with lethal anaesthetic drugs. I can't help feeling that he saw those drugs as symbolic – they represented the lost contract with Grange Hospital, and were intimately associated with his business failure.'

'I think there's another symbol that didn't escape him,' said Montgomery.

'There is?'

'Aside from the omission of potassium chloride, those are the drug classes used for judicial executions in the United States.'

They wandered to Vicars' Court, the pleasant residential quadrangle, then turned back along the south side of the Minster. Montgomery paused by an ivy-covered sarcophagus. 'You missed something,' he said. 'Those ten-thirty sightings of Robert outside the pharmacy. He was going to post his letter. I realized that this morning once I'd decided to focus on Robert again.'

'Yes – you said you'd tell me how you concluded it was him. He *was* on the video, but you already knew what you were looking for.'

Montgomery indicated a door in the wall behind them,

165

alongside a clutch of weathered gargoyles. A sign said 'Refectory'. 'Let me buy you a coffee,' he said. 'Then I'll tell you.'

'I was reading *Lord of the Flies*,' said Montgomery.

'Good book, that.'

Their table was discreetly situated in the corner of the Minster's small tea-room. William Bird took an approving bite of chocolate caramel shortbread while Montgomery continued, 'There was a boy called Piggy, remember? The one who tried to do things properly. Quite early on he made me think of Robert McPherson, because both wore thick glasses and would be helpless without them. We'd found spectacles on the corpse and wondered if Robert had left them behind as a blind – no pun intended. In the event, not only did a second pair exist, but the body did turn out to be that of Robert himself.

'This morning, while I was grappling with grave doubts about Geoff Crabbe as our suspect, I happened to pick up the book and notice that Piggy's eye problem was described as "myopia". That was an honest mistake of Golding's. If Piggy had been myopic, his glasses would have been useless for starting fires.'

'There was a film version a few years back,' interjected William Bird. 'They made all the children American, with some truly horrible slang. But it was basically a good effort, and the spectacle lenses were convex – I can remember the scene where they lit the fire.'

'Exactly. They corrected the error. But the book this morning made me stop and think. Robert was short-sighted, and so is his mother. The first time we met her I registered vaguely the fact that her eyes looked small behind the lenses, but after that – well, it's the kind of thing you notice and then forget about, isn't it?

'This morning, though, I thought about it again. Honour claimed her glasses had started the old fire in the summer

166

house. But that was physically impossible. So why had she said that? I could think of only two reasons: either she was labouring under a misapprehension, or she felt the need to lie.

'Why should she lie? It could only have been to lead us away from any possible connection with Robert. Which in turn had to mean that she knew, or at the very least suspected, that Robert had fired his own pharmacy. I felt that she knew. There had been a marked change in Honour's demeanour between our first and second visits: the second time she looked terribly shocked and haggard, as if she had only just been made aware of the tragedy. What might account for that dramatic difference? A letter . . . It was Wednesday morning, just the time when something posted second class on Saturday night might be expected to arrive. What other clues were there in Honour's behaviour? We all noticed that *she* was the person who rang every day asking for updates on the investigation, rather than Theresa. That wasn't grotesque hypocrisy. She was ringing to assure herself that we weren't about to charge some innocent person.'

'That's right,' said Sergeant Bird. 'On one of our visits she asked us if we had any suspects, and I got the distinct impression she was afraid of the answer.'

Montgomery concurred. 'The concept of a letter', he went on, 'fitted neatly with Robert's absence from the pharmacy at ten thirty. There's no post office in the Furlong End precinct, and the nearest post box is in the residential area just up the road beyond the car-park. That's the direction in which the two witnesses saw him walking.

'So what might Robert's motive have been for both suicide and arson? We'd already considered the fact that his business was doing badly, his wife was possibly having an affair, he was being blackmailed by Geoff Crabbe . . . but if he had a personal history of fire-raising, that gave a whole new complexion to the case. His actions on the day of his death seemed to indicate that something had upset him in Honour's house. Could it have been something about that old fire? At first the idea seemed a long shot, but then I remembered how Vera Blenkinsop had emphasized a build-up of tragedies within the McPherson family . . . I began to wonder, and trawl for more evidence. We hadn't solved the mystery of that little cup. It was a very special child's toy, too feminine to be Robert's, the wrong era to have been Isabel's. Might there have been another child? When Vera spoke of "Bella" we assumed she meant Isabel. Supposing that hadn't been the case? In my arrogance I'd cut her off without finding out. That was reprehensible.

'As you know, I went to St Michael's churchyard and found Bella. The date of her death corresponded with Margaret Kendall's comment that the summer-house fire happened "two or three years after Isabel died". Not proof of Robert's guilt, maybe, but highly suggestive, coupled with the fact that Honour had concealed Bella's existence from us. And the elder McPhersons, both keen gardeners, seemed to have un-characteristically given away land which had been in the family for generations . . .

'So what about opportunity? The Nottingham arsonist struck during evenings and weekends, on random days of the week. Could Robert have spent hours away from his home without people wondering where he was? The answer is yes. He only had to tell Theresa that he would be visiting Honour, and he knew she would never telephone to check. Wherever he kept his supply of paraffin, he was careful never to let it spill into the car or on to his clothes, so Theresa was none the wiser . . .

'Our evidence was all circumstantial, even the fire brigade video, but I felt that if we challenged Honour directly, she would prefer to tell the truth. And now we have Robert's letter . . .'

William Bird lovingly swallowed his last mouthful of coated shortbread and contemplated the table for a few moments. 'It's a pity he didn't seek help,' he said. 'I dare say drugs or psychotherapy might have broken the cycle.'

'The compulsion to light fires, maybe,' agreed Montgomery. 'But that was only part of the story. Robert's real quest was atonement.'

Outside once more in the sunshine, the two detectives made their way round to the Minster's west front with its square Norman design surmounted by unusual lead spires, more Rhenish in character than English. 'Fire is an ever-present hazard,' said William Bird thoughtfully. 'Did you know that the south spire here was set ablaze by lightning in 1711? The flames got a good hold thanks to high winds and jackdaw nests, and the bells came crashing down. Ironically, it was Guy Fawkes' Night.' He strode a few more feet, then stopped, turning to Montgomery. 'Geoff Crabbe went out of his way to invite suspicion by bolting,' he said. 'Why did he do that?'

'Oh, I think several factors played a part,' answered Montgomery. 'His own colleagues knew about the ten o'clock appointment, and it was quite conceivable that McPherson himself had told someone else, perhaps while discussing his difficulties in confidence. When McPherson deferred the meeting, Crabbe had no reason to tell anyone at that point; he simply spent more time with his mistress than he had anticipated having. He had already told Monica not to wait up.

'Next morning, however, he heard about the fire and missing pharmacist on the local radio. In a state of agitation he left Shona and drove to the area to have a look. He was horrified by what he saw, even more so when a local newsagent told him that a body had just been found. With a criminal record like his, which included threatening behaviour, he reasoned that the investigation was bound to be biased against him. Like most bullies, Geoff is essentially a coward, and on that Sunday he panicked. He drove to the cottage and decided to keep a low profile until more facts had emerged.

'With fevered imaginings of phone taps and the like, he felt that direct contact with Monica was too risky. Unwisely, he chose Sean to relay a cover story to her, and to keep him

169

posted on the police investigation. Geoff would ring out from the mobile at prearranged times, but otherwise keep the machine switched off to block any incoming calls.

'As we know, Sean thought Geoff was guilty. Why not? It was the kind of thing he might have done himself. But the situation had turned Geoff into a liability. There wasn't time to destroy all the evidence of Geoff's more nefarious dealings at the barn; Sean didn't know every place to look, and new consignments were imminently expected. It was safer to play the innocent dupe helping to run Morgifts.

'But *Geoff* knew Sean's degree of involvement. He also knew Sean was a minor drug pusher, not just a user. If Geoff could be silenced, Sean would not only be off the hook, he could make use of Geoff's many contacts and build up his own enterprise. At least, he thought he could. Personally, I have my doubts. In the long run, cunning is no substitute for intelligence.'

'What do you think about Andrew?'

'Andrew? A rather pathetic young man badly out of his depth. Whatever dishonesties led to his sacking by Robert McPherson, Andrew is strictly small-time.'

'Andrew, take this to the chemist for me, will you? You might be out of a job but you don't have to sit on your backside all day!' Andrew Dunster's mother thrust her prescription into his pudgy hand and shooed him towards the front door. Sulkily, he lumbered out into the street. It was true that he did need employment soon – he was running out of spending money. All he knew was how to be a pharmacy assistant, but that didn't pay as well as he would like . . . after a suitable period of time he planned a reversion to making a little 'extra' with prescription charges . . .

At the pharmacy a female dispenser he knew slightly glanced at the doctor's scrawl, then flipped the script over. 'This isn't for you,' she stated.

'No – for my mother.'

'She hasn't signed.'

'I know – we pay.'

'Ah, right.' She took his cash. 'Could you sign the bottom, please? Sorry about the inconvenience. It's the new rules to prevent fraud. Silly, isn't it, when we all know each other?'

Andrew felt his face go slack. As if in a dream, he felt his hand grip the proffered pen and inscribe his name.

'Shame about your pharmacy burning down,' she went on. 'Have you got another job yet?'

'Not right now.'

'Well, don't you worry. You know what they say. "As one door closes . . ." '

He flung the pen down. *So does another*, he thought.

'Self-injection needn't necessarily be performed via a needle,' said Ian May to the two detectives. 'If Robert McPherson had used a cannula, for instance, he'd have required a needle for the initial insertion but then discarded it, leaving only plastic components *in situ*.'

'Which would melt,' said William Bird.

'Yes. And if he really wanted to minimize the chance of someone finding out, he might have used a vein near the foot. Look, I'll show you . . .' He lifted his left foot on to an adjacent chair, rolled up the trouser leg and pushed down the sock. He then grasped the lower calf tightly, just above the ankle. 'Pretend my hand's a tourniquet,' he said. 'See that vein?' A thin blue streak was beginning to swell in front of the medial malleolus, the inner 'ankle bone'. Briskly he tapped at the overlying skin, and the distension increased.

'Using a tourniquet, Robert would have had both hands free,' he went on, releasing his grip and restoring his clothing to its former state of neatness. 'And there's an additional advantage to choosing the ankle – it's further from the heart than is, say, the forearm. Drugs injected at a lower limb site would take longer to reach the arterial circulation, hence longer to take effect.'

'Ah,' said Montgomery. 'Less chance of losing consciousness before the injection was complete.'

'Indeed. There might even have been time for him to throw his cannula, or butterfly needle or whatever, right across the room.' He paused to remove a booklet, *Population Trends*, from a nearby shelf. 'Did you know that in these records pharmacists come out as the second most likely group of men to commit suicide, with dentists, farmers and doctors close behind? Only vets have a greater risk, maybe because putting down creatures in distress is an integral part of their culture. But the key point is drugs availability . . . Access to something lethal before you have a chance to reflect and change your mind.'

Six months later Montgomery, wearing his smartest dark suit and most sober silk tie, made a thankful exit from headquarters and strode towards his parked car as rapidly as dignity would allow.

'Dad,' whined Justin, all of fifteen. 'Just one picture, *please*. You did it for *them*.'

'There wasn't a lot of choice,' came the reply.

'Just one for our album,' begged Heather, two years younger. 'You and Mum, and the certificate.'

'The light's not very good. I think you'll find . . . ' He paused, and relented. 'All right. But quickly.' He turned in time to see the eager pride on their faces before they bent smooth raven-black heads to the intricacies of camera settings. In the background William Bird was grinning broadly. 'I still think you had something to do with this,' Montgomery accused him. 'Despite your promise to keep quiet about Bishop Street.'

'This' was the ceremony of the day, during which he had received a Chief Constable's Commendation, a hearty handshake before the assorted flash units of the local press, two

172

soggy vol-au-vents and a glass of Perrier; he had experienced both pleasure and embarrassment in roughly equal measure.

'Not guilty,' insisted the sergeant. 'Well, not directly, anyway. It was Annie Bartholomew's doing. I just smoothed her path.'

'All the way to the Super's in-tray.'

'Mm . . . broadly speaking, yes. But she wrote the initial note. I believe it took someone half a day to decipher it. Then enquiries were made, details established. You know how it is . . .'

Montgomery straightened his back as Heather signalled her readiness. He stood with Carole, holding the certificate out for inspection as if it were an item of evidence, as in a sense it was. He wished he had the Chief Constable's easy poise in front of cameras.

'Smile!' called out Justin.

Montgomery reluctantly obliged, and the wintry afternoon was bejewelled with flashes of light. He posed for the inevitable extra shots with good grace, then joined William Bird as his sergeant prepared to return to the building. 'How is Annie?' Montgomery asked him. 'Have you seen her recently?'

'Oh, you know Annie, sir. She wouldn't stay in the hostel beyond that first week. Loves her freedom, even if her lifestyle might seem squalid to you and me . . . Someone spotted her at the Goose Fair back in October, but now? She's moved on. She might be in Mansfield, or Derby.'

'By rights she should have been here today.'

'Don't worry. She knew you were going to get an award. She was determined that would happen.'

Carole and the two teenagers approached, still discussing photographs. 'I saw the man from the *Recorder*,' she said to Montgomery. 'If they print a good picture I shall write and ask for a copy.'

'I wonder what the caption will be?' mused Heather.

'I can suggest to them an apposite one,' said William Bird.

They looked at him expectantly. As Justin urged, 'Go on,' the heavily built sergeant glanced towards Montgomery and prepared for flight.

'*Modesty Blaze*,' he said.

4/97